BEGINNINGS

Laura Phillips

A KISMET™ Romance

METEOR PUBLISHING CORPORATION
Bensalem, Pennsylvania

KISMET™ is a trademark of Meteor Publishing Corporation

First Printing October 1992.

ISBN: 1-56597-025-X

Printed in the United States of America.

With thanks to Nora for helping me understand what I have not experienced.

And to Ronnie, whose short life enriched my own.

LAURA PHILLIPS

Laura Phillips is a former reporter and news editor who once couldn't imagine settling for motherhood. Now she can't imagine her life without the happy chaos created by her three children and their assorted pets. She and her husband make a home for the entire crew in Kansas City, Missouri. When she isn't writing or doing Mommy jobs, she can be found in the backyard garden.

Other books by Laura Phillips:

No. 22 *NEVER LET GO*
No. 40 *CATCH A RISING STAR*
No. 78 *TO LOVE A COWBOY*
No. 99 *MOON SHOWERS*

ONE

The closed windows of the general office building trapped the air-conditioning, creating a cool haven. But they barely muted the thunder of the roller coaster car whipping past on the wooden track not a hundred feet away. Abby Monroe pressed a blunt-nailed finger against one ear to stifle the sound while she cradled the receiver against the other and strained to hear over the brief cacophony.

The ringing at the other end of the line ceased as Dad's answering machine clicked on. The taped John Wayne imitator launched into the long spiel that preceded the beep.

"Damn!" she muttered. Dad thought the message had character. Abby thought it was irritating, especially now when she didn't have a moment to waste. She shifted uncomfortably and glanced around the tile-floored personnel office while waiting for the canned message to end. Brett Holland, the general manager, paused in the open doorway. He moved on when he saw it was only Abby borrowing the desk and phone.

Finally, the phony Duke finished. "Come on, Dad. Pick up the phone if you're there. It's important." She hesitated, wondering if he really had left. He hadn't spoken to her since their argument yesterday afternoon. Most likely, he didn't know what to say.

"Well, call me at work as soon as you can. Please. My car broke down. I need to borrow yours. You could pick me up at three o'clock. That would give me time to drop you off at home again and make it to the—" A loud insistent beep interrupted. The machine clicked, buzzed, and disconnected her.

Damned machine. She hated it. Worse, she hated to have to ask Dad for anything just now. A thirty-three-year-old woman shouldn't have to beg for the family car keys.

With a frustrated sigh, she replaced the receiver. She didn't think he would call, not if he was still angry with her. She racked her brain for another source of transportation. Most of her co-workers either carpooled, rode the bus, or had their parents drop them off. Of course, there were always her sisters. But Maureen had to pick the kids up after school. And environmentally conscious Bethany had ridden with her carpool again today.

Abby wondered if the clinic was close to the bus line. Or maybe, by some miracle, the dealership's repair department could fix her car a lot faster than estimated. No, that was too much to hope for.

Put it out of your mind. Closing her eyes, she breathed in deeply. She had to relax or the dolphins would pick up on her tension. They'd be too skittish to perform, which would reflect badly on her as a trainer. And she couldn't afford any setbacks now, not when everything was going according to schedule. Almost everything, she corrected herself, remembering her car. The breakdown was an inconvenience, a major one. At least it had occurred within a mile of the theme park, so she hadn't had to walk too far. That much was a blessing, considering the city was experiencing another classic midwestern humid heat wave. Speaking of blessings, the car was still under warranty, so there wouldn't be any big repair bills to eat into her carefully managed budget.

A loud tap on the half-open door startled her out of her thoughts. The small, lean woman didn't wait for an answer as she slipped inside and closed the door behind her.

"Done with my desk?"

"Almost, Bethany." Abby dug around in the center drawer until she found a pencil. "Holland was here looking for you a minute ago."

Her sister grimaced as she slid her lithe runner's body into the chair opposite Abby and slapped the stack of file folders onto the desk.

"He caught up with me in the copy room. The big guy's in a panic over some troubleshooter the home office is sending over. He wants reports from all the departments, ASAP, as in yesterday. What are you looking for now?"

Abby quit rummaging through the hopeless clutter on top of the desk. "Something to write on. I need to leave a note with instructions for the tow truck. My car? Remember?"

"Third drawer on the left. Did you reach Dad?"

The pencil halted, then resumed its mad dance across the page. "I left a message. Since I'm not there to growl at, he's probably out in the yard torturing the petunias. Gotta go. Lunch?"

Bethany tapped the stack of files pointedly, hesitating

an instant before answering. "After your twelve thirty show?"

"See you then." Abby ripped the top sheet off the notepad and folded it as she slipped around the desk.

"Abby, wait!"

"I can't. I have a show in—eight minutes," she said, checking her waterproof wristwatch.

"Maybe the repair shop can loan you something to drive."

"I already asked. Both their loaners are already out."

"One more thing," Bethany interjected. "Do you want me to talk to Dad?".

Abby shook her head. "It wouldn't do any good. You'd end up fighting with him, too. He'll eventually get used to the idea, just like he adjusted when I dropped out of premed to major in theater. And when you took off to Belize with that archaeologist."

"Dad loves you. He only wants what's best for you."

Abby smiled wistfully. She knew her sister was right. "We have different ideas about what that is."

"I'll talk to him."

"Don't," Abby insisted, shooting her a stern look as she cleared the doorway. Heading down the hall at a half run, Abby barely stopped for a quick word with the receptionist. The woman took the note and ignition key, promising to pass them on to the tow truck driver when he showed up.

Once out the door, she jogged around the building and along a curved path through the trees. She slipped through a maze of shrubbery, fences, and passageways to emerge outside one of the two employee dining rooms in the park. Beyond that was the French Quarter district, loosely modeled after the historic section of

New Orleans. Dodging groups of park visitors, she made her way past the wax museum, the Octopus, and the Riverboat Restaurant to the California Shores section, where the dolphin pool was located.

A quick glimpse around the corner told her the amphitheater was already half filled, and visitors were still streaming through the gates. Quickly, she slipped through the back door, through the narrow passageway between plastic barrels of pool chemicals. She paused at the head of the stairs leading down into the workroom, giving her eyes a chance to adjust to the dimmer light before tackling the sometimes slippery stairs. She'd already kicked off her street shoes when she noticed the workroom lights blazing.

The ushers must have come looking for her. They were probably in a panic because she hadn't shown up yet. Well, there wasn't time to reassure them. She flung her shoes into a corner and skipped down the steps. She was nearly at the bottom when she saw the stranger. She halted, clutching the railing in her surprise.

Silhouetted against the tall white of the upright freezer was a walking advertisement for Italian suits. The trim cut of the fabric outlined broad shoulders and tapered to a set of narrow hips encased in pleated trousers that, for all their looseness, gave the impression of lean athleticism. Or perhaps it was the man's stance, all brisk, impatient energy in search of an outlet. Hearing her approach, he turned and fixed her with a questioning look. His long fingers fiddled with his sunglasses while gracing her with a wide, appreciative grin.

"Can I help you?" she asked, pasting on her "welcome to the park" smile. Another handsome but wayward tourist who thought the "employees only" signs didn't apply to him. Except this one wasn't dressed for the part. Even the most uptight weekend fathers managed to loosen up enough for a sports shirt and duck twills. The intruder's well-made gray suit and starched white shirt looked ready to wilt from the heat, much like the rest of him. Sweat beaded his high forehead, dampening the honey brown hair draped loosely over his temples and half hiding his ears.

He glanced around the room, then back at her, his expression self-deprecating. "I must have taken a wrong turn. I've lost the others. This is the office for the dolphin pool?"

Abby shot him a dubious look. In no way could the damp pit of exposed pipes and equipment be deemed an office. He was stalling, probably hoping to indulge his curiosity a bit longer. Well, she didn't have time for this. She'd direct him back out the way he'd come, pleasantly and politely, just as the park policy dictated.

"I'm sorry, but your party isn't likely to find you here. This is a restricted area. Employees only. You didn't see the signs?"

"I'm sure this is the place. In fact, I'm positive," he replied, slanting her a thorough glance. "Brett must have been delayed. I'm Matt Gardner from the—"

"Like I said, Mr. Gardner, this area is off-limits to visitors. How *did* you get in here?" she asked, trying to temper her irritation. The ushers were supposed to watch all the exits to keep this sort of thing from happening. Explanations were in order, and she'd damn sure have them after the show.

"I came in the way you did. The door wasn't locked," he said in a tone that implied it should have been. "What's this?" he continued, stepping up onto a narrow wooden platform to peer down into the dolphin pool filter.

"Filtration equipment," she retorted, heading back up the stairs. "Can you find your own way out or do you need help?'' She stopped by the phone, three steps down from the pit entrance. In two seconds, she could call security to remove him, except it would take them a few minutes to get here, and a while longer for explanations, protests, and so forth.

He stepped off the platform and turned toward her. Finally he was leaving.

''Can I wait in here?'' he asked, dashing her hopes. Abby reached for the phone.

It rang beneath her fingertips, startling her. She threw him an angry glance and snatched up the receiver.

''Dolphin pool, Abby Monroe speaking.''

''You called?'' Jake Monroe's cool tone disappointed her. He was still angry with her.

''Yes, Dad,'' she said, turning to face the wall. The man's watching eyes made her edgy. ''About the car?''

''What about the car? Why do you need it?''

Abby stifled the urge to scream and threw a surreptitious glance over her shoulder. ''I can't go into detail now. We discussed it last night. We've been discussing it for days. Remember?'' Dad knew about her appointment, and he certainly didn't approve. That's why he was being so obtuse. But she couldn't cancel, not at the optimum point in her cycle.

''I don't have time to discuss it now,'' she said. ''Are you going to give me a ride or not?''

A breathy sigh ending in a snort sounded through the receiver. ''I'll pick you up. What time?''

''Three. I have to be at the clinic by three thirty. I can drop you off at home on the way. Thanks, Pop.''

Abby hung up the receiver before her father could change his mind or even suggest further discussion. Her stomach was already churning with nervousness. She didn't need her father's doubts and recriminations.

She spun around to face the man who was now nosing through the freezer.

"What are you doing?" she demanded.

"You'd rather I got out of your hair, I suppose. You have a show in a few minutes, don't you?" he asked, closing the freezer door. He took one step toward her, then another. One polished leather shoe landed in the perpetually wet spot at the bottom of the steps. His foot skidded out from under him. He grabbed wildly at the banister, clutched, and lost his grip as he thumped to the hard floor with a loud grunt.

Abby froze in horror, the specter of damage claims and lawsuits springing immediately to mind, courtesy of the warnings issued at the last safety meeting.

"Are you hurt?" she called, hurrying back down the steps. She leaned over to help him up, but he waved her away.

"I'll manage," he retorted. "I got myself down here. I'll get myself back up." He balanced, elbows on his knees, his color high. The unmistakable sound of a ripping seam halted his movement.

"That was an auspicious ending to an unforgettable moment," he muttered, struggling to rise. Abby covered her lips to stifle the giggle threatening to break free. Comic relief in an unexpected form. It broke the tension gripping her.

"You might have warned me about the floor," he said in a low, rueful tone.

"Are you sure you aren't hurt?"

"Quit hovering. I'm fine," he muttered, shrugging out of his jacket and inspecting it. Other than a damp spot on the tail, it seemed no worse for the wear. He turned around, slinging the jacket over the low freezer in the corner. Abby held her breath, expecting to see a wide expanse of white exposed in the back center seam of his well-fitted trousers. Or maybe bright red, or even a jungle print. Anyone who wore that board room costume with overgrown, untamed hair like his had a rebellious streak.

"Will you look at that?"

"Look at what?" she stuttered. Her face flamed as she turned and retrieved a bucket of fish from the refrigerator.

"My shirt, of course. Do you think it can be fixed?"

Abby twisted around to stare at his back. He'd turned around to display the torn seam gaping low on the shoulder. The shirt fit his body like a handmade glove, tapering around his narrow waist and disappearing into the trousers. Her gaze traveled lower, taking in the chiseled, narrow hips molded against the clinging wet fabric.

"Well?" he asked.

Abby jerked back around and grabbed the scale. "How should I know? Ask your tailor." He had to have one. You couldn't buy clothes like that off the rack. It was just her luck to get stuck with a meddlesome clotheshorse now of all times.

She dumped a handful of herring into the tray to measure out the two pounds she'd need. There was barely enough. She'd have to thaw more before the next show.

The show.

She hoisted the bucket from the sink's drain board and turned to the man. "Please," she began. "You have to leave. Company policy. No visitors in the work area. You could get me fired." *There*, she thought. *That ought to do it.* Already, she could see the softening, the faint stirrings of guilt and regret in his expression.

The door swung open, and the older of the teenage

ushers poked his head inside. "Hey, Abby! Get a move on. We have a full house, and they're getting restless."

"Coming!" she replied.

"One more thing. The water level dropped really low this morning. When you didn't show up, I went ahead and added more the way you showed me. You might want to double-check the chemical mix after the show," he said.

"Thanks, just what I needed, another problem," she said, then winced when the door slammed shut with an echoing bang.

"Why don't you wait outside on the steps? Or better yet, watch the show. Otto and Pepper are pretty talented," she said.

"Maybe later. I'd better do something about these clothes," he said, tugging his jacket on as he started up the stairs ahead of her.

The dark wet stain barely showed beneath the jacket tail, looking no worse than if someone had sat on a damp bench. Abby dragged her eyes higher, focusing on the back of his head. "I wouldn't worry," she said. "Nothing much shows with your jacket on. And around here, people are always getting wet anyway."

He stopped, shooting her a quizzical glance.

"The water rides. The Sawmill Chute, the Roaring River Rapids. And here at the dolphin pool we call the first couple of rows the designated splash zone. Of course, most people dress a bit more casually. You, on the other hand, look like a Wall Street broker."

He paused at the top of the steps and held the door open for her. "I came straight from an early board meeting in New York."

"To an amusement park?" She spied the usher down the corridor. He held up an arm and tapped his watch pointedly. She nodded and motioned him closer, pointing surreptitiously at Mr. Gardner. She didn't trust the man not to slip back into the pit and indulge his weird fascination for filtration equipment.

"I love amusement parks—good ones," Mr. Gardner said. He crinkled his nose as she passed. "Mmmm. Smells like brunch on the plane."

Abby grinned. Intruder or not, he had an odd sort of charm, especially when that little dimple appeared next to his smile. "Quite a day for you, too, huh?"

"It's just beginning." His somber tone dimmed the smile on his lips.

"That's what I'm afraid of," she said with a low groan. "Use the door on the left. It'll take you out next to the Snow Cone stand. There's a map of the park a few yards to your left after that."

Not waiting for his response, she reached around behind her and punched the button to start the tape machine. While the prerecorded introduction played over the speakers, she headed through the short, narrow corridor to the stage door.

A quick glance over her shoulder caught him easing through the exit. He gave her the high sign and closed the door behind him.

Abby quickly clipped on her microphone and took a deep breath. Seconds later, the canned introduction ended, signaling her entrance.

With a broad smile and a wave for the crowd, she stepped onto the wet, carpeted stage and hung the fish bucket from a hook on the rail. Then she launched into her routine, introducing Otto and Pepper.

When she reached the point where she revealed Pepper's weight, Pepper shook her head, squawking in a singsong tone, right on cue.

"What do you mean, no?" Abby retorted and signaled the next movement. Pepper repeated the head shake.

"What if I gave you this fish?" Abby held up a small herring. Pepper shook her head.

Abby dug in the bucket. "How about this one?" she said, holding up one three times the size of the first. Pepper nodded vigorously, then Otto joined in. Throwing them each a fish, Abby continued her monologue of facts about Atlantic bottle-nosed dolphins. With a flick of her right hand, she signaled them into their first series of leaps around the pool.

Watching them, she noticed the water level was still a bit low and made a mental note to add more as soon as the show finished. Then she introduced the first real trick, the "slow dance" she'd developed with these two last winter.

Otto and Pepper balked. Abby signaled again, but the dolphins playfully swam around the pool, then raised their snouts expectantly. But they still refused to respond to Abby's instructions.

"Sorry, folks," she said, pasting on a stage smile. "They're mad at me 'cause I didn't get their breakfast to them on time. They tend to forget that if they don't behave, they won't get any lunch at all. Right, children?" she added, directing the last to the bottle-nosed gray beaks protruding from the water near her feet. She signaled a nod and received a halfhearted response before they disappeared beneath the surface. They definitely weren't going to cooperate.

For several minutes, Abby took questions from the audience. Halfway through the third answer, she spied a somber-looking suit near the top of the arena. A second look confirmed it. Mr. Gardner had opted for the show after all.

After two more questions, Abby continued with the

show, skipping the dance. She tossed a regulation basketball into the water and held her breath until Otto nosed it up and circled the pool with it balanced on the tip of his snout. Pepper seemed more willing, too, immediately taking her turn in the opposite direction.

Two jumps later, Abby noticed the water level had dropped a good six inches lower still, and she shot a worried look over at the usher. With a nod, he headed for the pit while she continued. The water level was now too low to safely attempt the high jumps, so she decided to take a chance with the slow dance again. After a brief hesitation, Pepper and Otto nuzzled up, belly to belly, and eased across the pool.

Tossing out the requisite fish, she glanced over at the usher, who had reappeared. He shrugged. "Call maintenance," she mouthed, then looked out over the crowd.

"I need a volunteer, about so tall," she said, holding her hand a little higher than her waist. This was the part where she fed the audience a little scientific information mixed in with good-old-boy humor. Her partner, Jay, was better at the humor angle, but she'd managed to add a few touches of her own over the last five years.

Picking a little girl about seven years old, she launched into the routine. To her relief, the dolphins cooperated eagerly, while the child was just reluctant enough to make the jokes work. And when Abby came to the part where she cajoled the child into holding the fish by her teeth so Pepper could retrieve it, the girl predictably balked.

"Look, Becky. If I can do it, you can," Abby said. "Just be sure you use some mouthwash before you kiss your boyfriend." Abby demonstrated with the fish, and Otto edged up, snatching it with a quick movement.

As Abby backed away from the pool, her eyes were

drawn again to Matt Gardner. He was still there but no longer sitting alone. Brett Holland, the park manager, had joined him.

An uneasy chill danced down Abby's spine, outweighing even the slimy taste of fish scales. What had Gardner said? *Brett must have been delayed.*

Abby groaned inwardly, remembering the troubleshooter Bethany had mentioned earlier. Ten to one he was the man Abby had kicked out of the pit. She suspected her trouble had only begun, and just when she needed to be calm and tranquil.

How was she supposed to conceive a child this afternoon when everything else was going wrong?

TWO

Matt had to admit that the woman had moxie. She was definitely more of a performer than those porpoises in the pool. In fact, he was beginning to wonder if their apparent reluctance to obey her commands wasn't just another part of the performance, an ingenious trick to milk the audience for sympathy and for laughs.

She'd handled him nearly as well, too, kicking him out of her domain firmly but with uncommon good nature. He wondered where the performance ended and the woman behind it began. It might be interesting to find out, assuming his work kept him here long enough for more than a casual dinner squeezed between phone calls and meetings. It might be interesting to know whether her lips were really as soft and kissable as they looked.

Then she put the fish in her mouth. Matt nearly choked on his thoughts.

A tap on his shoulder jarred his attention from the routine, and Matt was grateful for the distraction.

"What kept you, Holland?" he asked, moving down the bench to make room for the park manager.

"Sorry. Phone call from Atlanta. Seems you really shook them up down there," Brett replied.

Matt kept his tone neutral. "I made a few recommendations. The operation was in pretty good shape already." He caught Brett's uneasy nod out of the corner of his eye and suppressed a smile. He'd counted on the corporate grapevine to frighten the complacency out of the manager. Apparently, he'd been right again.

He kept silent as Abby abandoned the fish routine and asked the child if she was ready for a boat ride. The little girl practically danced with anticipation as she eyed the small raft perched at the edge of the pool.

"This one's a real crowd pleaser," Brett commented. "The kids love it and so do the parents. How many kids can say they've been towed by a dolphin?"

Matt didn't answer.

"We were concerned at first about the liability question, but our insurers passed on the act, so I suppose there's nothing to worry about. Even if the kid falls in, she's perfectly safe with the life jacket on. And the dolphins are harmless."

"The sign says they bite." He watched Abby secure the child in the raft, then toss the pull ring to the dolphin she called Otto.

"Some do. Mainly, though, the sign keeps visitors from trying to pet them."

"And subsequently falling into the pool," Matt surmised with a nod. "This trainer handles the crowd well. Where did you find her?"

"Abby? It's kind of a coincidence, really. She's from the city originally, but she's been working in Mississippi. When Marine Shows got the dolphin contract here, she asked for a transfer—I guess to be closer to her family. Her sister's the personnel director. You'll meet Bethany later at the managers' meeting."

"Sounds like nepotism."

Brett stiffened. "Not really since we don't employ the trainers. Abby and Jay are on the Marine Shows payroll, not ours. Besides, what difference does it make? Both the Monroe women are damn good at their jobs, even if they are a little different." His voice rose at the end, drawing the attention of several people around them.

Matt lowered his sunglasses, peering at the park manager over the top. The man certainly was defensive. "I'd say anybody who puts a dead fish in her mouth is a little different," he replied carelessly, then turned back to the show. Otto was still circling the pool with the child in tow.

"Is this the last trick?"

"Just about. There's a couple of spectacular high jumps where the dolphins slap that balloon, Otto with his tail and Pepper with her nose," he said, pointing to the bright pink ball hanging about fifteen feet above the pool's surface.

"Sounds impressive." Matt tilted his chin, studying Abby as she tweeted the whistle hanging around her neck. Its high-pitched tone barely carried over the tiny microphone clipped to her collar, but one dolphin obeyed the call immediately. Otto didn't. He pulled the raft almost to the edge of the pool, where Abby waited with one hand outstretched to catch the rope. Then he whirled away for another loop around the pool, then a second and a third.

Matt glanced uneasily at the child's parents. They were laughing and waving at their giggling offspring.

"Looks like Otto's acting up today," Brett commented, sounding as disturbed as Matt felt.

"She had some trouble earlier, too," Matt informed him. "Maybe this is happening more than you think."

He focused on Abby, on the slight change in her voice and the stiffening of her shoulders. As a child, he'd learned to read people, to decipher emotions they tried to hide. Watching her, he no longer believed the dolphin's obstinacy was part of the routine.

From the stage, Abby teased the child, claiming the dolphin liked her so much that he wanted to keep her. She rambled on, covering the glitch with bits of information about the intelligence of dolphins and speculation about their sense of humor. "Damn, but she's good," Matt muttered. Aside from a faint stiffness that entered her loose-gaited walk, she appeared mostly unaffected by her charge's apparent defection.

Working the crowd, she signaled the dolphin again. Finally she persuaded the beast to give up the tow line. She helped the child back onto solid footing, then announced the end of the show and directed the crowd to the proper exits.

"What about the high jumps?" Matt asked, still watching her. She approached one of the ushers, listened a moment, then nodded and disappeared behind the stage door.

"I don't know," Brett replied, rising from his seat. "Something's up. She's supposed to stick around to answer questions. If you don't mind waiting a few minutes, I'll go see what the problem is."

"I'll join you," Matt replied, following the general manager down the steps, weaving his way against the flow of the crowd.

Their progress was slow until they reached the arena floor. From there, it took less than a minute to circle around to the other side of the pool, cross the damp, nonskid carpeting on the stage, and slip through the stage door. Once inside, Abby's voice drifted up the passageway.

"I don't know what the problem is. I just know that the pool is dropping about an inch every five minutes. And that's quite a feat for a pool that doesn't even have a bottom drain," she said. "I've checked all the valves."

Her eyes widened in surprise when the two men came into view, then narrowed again as her fingers tightened on the telephone receiver. "*No, I don't think it can wait until after lunch.*" She turned and hung up with quick snapping motions.

"Idiots," she muttered.

"Problems?" Matt asked.

"In spades," she said over her shoulder as she hurried down the stairs. Turning a valve, she started a rush of water through the system. "Hang on a minute." She fiddled with another valve, flicked a couple of switches, then headed back upstairs. The laughing, amiable performer was gone now. Abby Monroe was all business and looking worried as a CEO with a strike pending.

"You might have told me who you were, instead of letting me think you were another one of our overly curious guests," she said as Matt stepped aside to let her pass.

"And that is?"

"I'd say you're from headquarters, probably the troubleshooter I heard about. If I hadn't been distracted earlier, I'd have realized it then." She stepped over to the door and glanced out, searching for an instant before turning back. "Well, am I right?"

"I tried to tell you, but you didn't let me finish. You seemed in a hurry to get your fish washed. Now I know why."

Abby fixed him with a challenging stare, though a hint of a smile teased at the corner of her lips. "I suppose this means dinner and a movie are out of the question?"

Holland cleared his throat. He glanced uncomfortably from one to the other. "I didn't realize you'd already met. Again, Matt, I apologize for being late."

"Actually, I'm grateful. I caught Miss Monroe off guard, and sometimes that can be quite revealing."

Laughter sparked in her eyes, though she contained it. *Bad choice of words, Gardner. She didn't reveal anything, but you showed how carelessly clumsy you could be.* Though his pants were nearly dry now, he could almost feel the cool squish again of the puddle he'd tumbled into. Her expression indicated she knew exactly what he was remembering. It irritated him that he could be so transparent. It was his job to keep other people off balance, not the other way around.

"The security here stinks," he said and watched the laughter die. The words needed to be said, but for the first time in years, he regretted his duty. He couldn't afford that brand of regret, though. The company couldn't afford it.

"I walked right in," he continued. "Nobody even noticed me, and I'm not exactly dressed to blend in with the crowd. Anybody could have come in here and tampered with the equipment, even me for all you know."

Abby started to protest, then hesitated at his stern expression. He was right. How many times had she complained to the part-time ushers about their lax attention? She'd thought exactly the same thing, even suspected him for an instant.

"It's possible," she conceded. "But more than likely, it's just another broken valve someplace."

"This has happened before?" Matt's narrowed glance

shifted between Abby and the park manager, who wiped at the sweat beads forming on his furrowed brow.

"The equipment is old," Brett explained. "It's bound to break down occasionally."

Abby stalked past him and glanced out the door again. "Occasionally?" She shot the manager a dark look. "For two years you've been talking renovations, but I have yet to see so much as a can of paint anyplace the visiting public can't see. We have two very valuable and very sensitive creatures in that pool, and these breakdowns are endangering their welfare. It's hard enough keeping the salt and chlorine and pH in balance under normal circumstances. But this is a nightmare. It's no wonder Otto and Pepper are feeling cantankerous today."

"Maintenance will be here soon enough," Brett soothed. "They'll find the leak."

Abby hesitated, lowering her voice. "That's not the point, and you know it."

"What is the point?" Matt interjected. Abby felt herself flush. She didn't like losing her temper in front of strangers. Heck, she hated losing control at all.

"Brett, could we continue this in private? Or would you rather discuss it with the Mississippi office?"

"I'm sure they might be more reasonable," Brett replied. "After all, we are complying with the terms of the contract with Marine Shows. So, Matt, what did you want to see next?" The older man turned away, dismissing Abby without a word.

"I want to know exactly what's bothering Ms. Monroe," Matt replied. "After all, my job here is to determine whether this park is salvageable or not. I can't do that unless I know everything there is to know."

The tension hung heavy in the air between them. Abby drew a deep breath, fighting the knot forming at the back of her neck. "Ask Mr. Holland," she said, checking the walkway for signs of the repair crew she'd requested. "We've discussed this often enough, he probably has the argument memorized by now. I know I do."

"Damn it, Abby," Brett retorted in a tone that drew her attention away from the sidewalk outside. His flushed face and the throbbing vein at his throat indicated that the recent rumors about the manager's supposed heart condition might have a basis in fact.

"You don't understand the position we're in," he continued. "We're in a recession. Attendance is way down, way below projections. Receipts are down. The money just isn't there for anything more than the bare necessities right now. We'll all be damn lucky if the park can stay open for the rest of the season."

Abby crossed her arms against her chest. She'd heard this argument several times before over the last few years. "You're exaggerating again, Brett."

"No, he's not." Matt's words sliced through the tension, leaving relative silence in their wake.

Abby drew a deep breath, then exhaled in a slow whistle. "I see. I guess I owe you an apology, Mr. Holland. However, it doesn't solve the immediate problem. So if you'll excuse me, I need to check the pool and make a few adjustments."

"I'll call maintenance and put a rush on this," Holland offered. "That much won't cost us anything extra."

Abby nodded, a hint of the smile returning. "Maybe they'll eat faster if they hear from you."

"And one more thing—" Matt interjected in a low tone as he leaned closer. Abby could feel the heat radiating from his body. The faint scent of cologne mingled with salty skin.

"What's that?" she asked warily. His nearness overwhelmed her, tripping her heart into an erratic beat. It made no sense that a stranger would affect her this way, but then her hormones were in overdrive today anyway.

"Where can I find a good tailor? I found another rip," he said.

She felt a flush climb up her neck and across her face as she inventoried the possible sites of the second tear. Over his shoulder, she spotted Brett's quizzical look, which changed quickly to comprehension, then speculation. "Ask the concierge at your hotel," she recommended sweetly, throwing the obvious in his face. Any seasoned traveler would know that. And any seasoned adult male would recognize the brush-off she'd just delivered, no matter what her hormones were screaming.

"Now why didn't I think of that?" His brown eyes danced with amusement.

"Jet lag?" she suggested, donning her most saccharine smile.

"Well, Abby," Brett called from the doorway. "Looks like I won't have to make that call after all. Your crew is here."

Matt stepped back, taking her breath with him. Then his grin widened. "Are you married?"

"No."

"Engaged or otherwise attached?"

"You could say that," she replied, her smile returning as she thought of that afternoon's appointment. Her plans for that day, for the next few years in fact, definitely fell into the otherwise attached category. She certainly didn't have time or energy to waste on a corporate shark who was looking for a little diversion while he was in town.

Disappointment registered faintly in the brown eyes,

then disappeared behind a thoughtful expression. "We'll talk again," he said. "About the dolphins, of course."

"Of course." Her facial muscles were starting to ache from maintaining the smile. It lasted as long as it took for them to pass through the door and close it behind them. The next second she was directing the repair crew into the pit. While they set to work, she dialed the home number of the other trainer. Jay deserved a little warning before he arrived for work later today.

"That's the third leak this season," Jay replied when Abby finished telling him all that had happened. "This routine is getting old."

"Right. There's not much we can do about it either, at least until we know more about what this Gardner guy is up to. I know attendance has been down some but not that badly. And it always picks up later in June after school has been out for a while. You don't suppose something else is afoot, like a buy-out or something like that?"

"You could have a point there. Why don't you pump your sister about it? Central Office always finds out before the drones," Jay replied.

Abby groaned. "You do have a way with words. I am not, nor will I ever be, somebody's drone. Not in this lifetime. Now are you going to get here on time, or are you going to make me late for my appointment?"

"I'll be there before the end of the next show."

"If there is one," Abby opined. "Right now I'm not too optimistic about the water situation."

Despite Jay's assurances to the contrary, Abby continued to doubt the crew's ability to repair the leak, or even locate it. She had to cancel the next show, and when Jay arrived, she threw him an I-told-you-so look.

He simply shrugged his well-tanned shoulders and

pulled swimming trunks from his bag. "Then I guess we can work on the hoop jump while we wait."

Abby shook her head. "Think again. The water level's two feet low now."

He cast her a disbelieving look and hurried up the stairs and down the corridor. Abby had barely reached the stage door when she heard his shouted expletive.

"Have you called Mississippi yet?" he yelled when she stepped through.

"Yep. And Gary said we have to handle it from this end. I believe it's called delegating authority," she said. "The guys inside claim they'll have it finished before three thirty this afternoon. I'm not holding my breath. And I can't wait around either. I have to meet Dad at the front gate."

Jay checked his watch. "You'd better get moving then. And don't forget to punch out."

Abby sneered over her shoulder. The time clock was another of Brett Holland's irritating policies. She and Jay weren't even on the park's payroll, but Holland still insisted they turn in punched time cards every week. For company records, he claimed. Abby found it insulting and petty, particularly when both trainers had found it necessary to take on maintenance and even usher duties to cover shortfalls in Holland's staffing. That's something she'd like to pass along to Matt Gardner. And she'd already clued in Gary and his superiors in the Mississippi office. They'd have to be a bit more specific about AmericaLand's obligations in the next contract. If there was one.

The thought was sobering enough that Abby didn't notice the man standing in the pit entrance until she nearly ran into him.

"There you are," Matt said, reaching out to steady

her as she tottered from the abrupt halt. "How are the repairs going?"

"They aren't," she replied, slipping past him. He followed her downstairs, stepping over a dismantled section of pipe. He spoke to one of the crew members for a minute, then joined Abby over in the corner.

"He said they've narrowed it down to one of two valves. However, the best they can manage is to maintain the status quo until tomorrow when the part comes in," Matt explained.

"So I heard. However, both valves might be bad for all we know, which could take another day or two. This place is in rotten shape," Abby retorted, then bit her lip. She hadn't meant to say that much, not until she talked to Bethany and listened to her assessment of the man and his mission. Her sister was in a better position to judge what was really going on.

"Look, I'm in a hurry. I know this is a bad time to leave, but I have an appointment I can't cancel. I'll introduce you to Jay. He can tell you anything you need to know."

She started up the stairs, with Matt close on her heels.

"You lied to me," he said, the instant they crossed the threshold and passed out of the workmen's earshot.

"What?" Abby spun around, her voice squeaking with surprise.

"Hey, Abby. Who's the suit?" Jay strolled down the corridor into the cramped room. Dressed in a nylon running suit, he appeared the carefree opposite of Matt Gardner. He even walked with the easy, rolling gait of a man with few responsibilities and no worries. Jay took life as it came and didn't concern himself with what passed him by. He was having too much fun with what he had.

Abby hesitated, trapped between one man's outrageous assertion and the other's curious gaze. Throwing a furious glance Matt's way, she bit back the retort on the tip of her tongue. Common sense told her she'd be better off settling this in private. Or better yet, ignoring it altogether. Smart women didn't tangle with sharks.

"Jay, meet Matt Gardner. Matt, this is the man you need to talk to. And Jay, I'll call you when I'm finished."

"Right," he answered, shoving his hands into his pockets and rocking on his heels. "So what can I do for you, Mr. Gardner?"

"Nothing just now," Matt insisted. "Abby, wait up."

"I don't have time." She hurried out the door and down the steps.

"I'll walk with you." He easily matched her step for step, though she moved just shy of a trot. Blast the man, anyway. Why couldn't he just wait until tomorrow to bother her with his questions and analysis of all their collective shortcomings?

"Do I have a choice?" she asked, not bothering to conceal her irritation.

"Not really. Why did you mislead me?" he asked.

"I didn't know I had," Abby replied, stealing a look at his expression. He wore a serious, measuring look. "Perhaps you misunderstood. Care to be more specific so I can correct the error?"

"I checked your file. You're not married."

"I told you that," she interrupted.

"—and you also said you were attached. I have it on good authority that you aren't involved with anyone but your family and those porpoises. You led me to believe otherwise."

"That's what's bothering you?"

"I much prefer honesty."

Abby turned down the narrow path behind the Octopus with its load of screaming adolescents. "I was being tactful," she said over the noise. "But if you want perfect honesty, try this. I don't give my phone number to strangers, and I don't play around with traveling businessmen. I'm not interested in fun and games." Another turn and they were behind the employee dining room nearest the gate.

"That's all right. I can get your number from your personnel file if I need it," he said, following his words with a smug smile. "Your address, too. But it's much more interesting just listening to what they have to say at the coffee machine and in the copy room."

"That's just gossip," Abby retorted.

He chuckled, then held a door wide for her as she slipped outside the employee entrance toward the winding path through the trees. Abby went a few steps more before she glanced over at him. He still wore the smug grin.

"Well, what did you hear?" she finally asked.

"Your hours have been erratic this year, and rumor has it that you're working a second job, having an affair, or having false teeth implanted during all those afternoons you've taken off."

"Teeth?"

"They look fine to me. I'd leave them as they are if I were you. Or are these the new ones?"

"Mr. Gardner, if you came to speak to me about my teeth or any other half-baked stories you've been listening to or, more likely, making up, then you're wasting my time and the company's money. I'm sure you could put yourself to more productive use."

"You're right. Have dinner with me. We can talk

about the dolphins and the renovations you'd like to see. Strictly business."

The man didn't miss a beat, she thought. "Thanks, but I have plans. We can talk at the park between shows."

"I might be busy. Tonight, at least, I'm free."

"I'm not. But I'd be happy to come in early tomorrow if it'll help you with your scheduling," she offered.

"Ahh, an evening with this so-called attachment of yours." A hint of regret tinged his expression before fading into the detached, assessing look again.

"That's a pretty good guess," she replied. It wasn't at all what he implied, but in a sense her so-called attachment had her tied up for the evening. Heck, she'd be up half the night explaining things to Dad. If he even cared to listen. Dinner with this pushy man would be more pleasant.

"Too bad," he said. "You're interesting. You're the only woman I know with enough moxie to put a dead fish in your mouth."

Abby laughed. "And that's interesting?"

"You have great legs."

She shook her head, still amused. "Well, my legs and I thank you. Now I have to go. My ride's coming down the drive."

"All right. In the meantime, I *could* put a little pressure on Holland to hurry those repairs along."

"You'd even resort to bribery, wouldn't you?" she replied, startled at his persistence. In truth, she was a bit flattered, but she'd never admit it to him. Pretending indignation was safer in the long run.

"Whatever works."

"Mister, if you can get my pool fixed today, I'll cook you dinner."

"Deal," Matt said, holding out his hand.

Abby hesitated, then caught the mocking glint in his eyes. "Deal," she said, shaking on it. The touch sent a tremor up her arm, playing havoc with those hormones again. And when he finally released her fingers, she wondered if she'd made a pact with the devil.

"See you soon," he said, spinning on his heel and striding determinedly toward the administration building.

Abby had to shake herself mentally. The man had charisma, she had to admit that. And he had a nice backside, too. The sound of Dad's horn brought her sharply back to reality, and she hurried toward the car.

"Who was that?" Dad asked when she climbed in. His craggy gray brows knit together over the rims of his glasses.

"A consultant. He had some questions about the dolphin pool," she said.

"Is he married?"

"I don't think so. How should I know?" It wouldn't be the first time a married man had pursued her. Somehow, she didn't think Matt Gardner was the type to cheat on his wife, if he had one. He seemed too bluntly honest for that kind of subterfuge.

"I suppose you could find out if you wanted to," he replied, easing the car back out into the slow-moving traffic and pointing it toward the highway.

"It doesn't much matter. He really isn't my type."

Her father's only answer was a low grunt, then a muttered curse at the driver of the candy-red sports car that cut him off.

"Where are you going, Dad?" He'd turned the station wagon south instead of north toward home. She'd only been joking when she'd suggested to Bethany that her father might mean to kidnap her until he could change her mind. Apparently she'd underestimated him.

"Dad!" she practically yelled. "Turn this car around, now."

"Isn't this the way to the clinic?" He eased the pressure on the gas pedal, and the old vehicle immediately slowed.

Abby's jaw dropped, then clamped closed.

"Well, isn't it? Regional General? Or did you change doctors again?"

"No, Dad. I mean, yes. Regional General's the right clinic."

"Fine." The car surged forward.

Abby sat in silence, considering the unexpected development until they left the highway and turned onto a busy boulevard snaking through the city's center.

"Why aren't you trying to talk me out of this?"

Dad eased the car to a stop at a red light, before he met Abby's eyes. "Can I talk you out of it?"

"No." That much she was sure of.

"That's what I thought." The light turned green and his attention returned to his driving.

"You don't approve."

"No. And I don't understand. But you're a grown woman and you're going to do what you want to anyway." He sounded calm, only faintly judgmental. Abby wasn't fooled. He'd used these tactics on her many times before, letting her think she'd made her own decision only to find later that he'd quietly led her in the direction he thought she should go. She just hadn't figured out what direction he was leading her in this afternoon.

He turned the car into the clinic's parking lot and stopped in front of the main entrance. "I'll park the car and meet you in the lobby."

"You don't have to stay."

He released a deep, long suffering sigh. "I sat

through your Sunday School pageants, your band concerts, and even that ridiculous engagement party your mother insisted on throwing. And when that didn't work out, I let you cry on my shoulder until I had to wring my shirt out to keep it from dripping on the carpet. After all that, you think I'd let you do this alone?''

Abby swallowed hard and blinked against the prickling tears. *Damn those hormones anyway*, she thought, blaming them for the rush of emotion that held her speechless.

''Now don't misunderstand me. I'll just be waiting outside in the reception room.''

''Thanks, Dad.'' Abby leaned across the bench seat to kiss him on the cheek. He pulled her close in a tight hug for an instant, then released her.

''Get out of the car, child, before they give that test tube to somebody else.''

''Dad, they don't use a test tube. They—''

''Please,'' he begged. ''Spare me the details.''

THREE

The sun was dipping toward the western horizon when Abby returned to the dolphin pool. Pop hadn't wanted her to come back, insisting that she rest to "recover." But rest wouldn't help this curious, unsettled feeling she'd had ever since she'd lain on the cold, sterile table this afternoon. She hadn't changed her mind. It just hadn't been what she expected, despite the briefings from her doctor. It had been cold, impersonal.

But if it gave her a child, it was worth it.

A fleeting picture of Matt Gardner's broad shoulders, untamed brown hair, and laughing brown eyes flashed through her mind, and the cold dissipated. The thought stole her breath as easily as his nearness had this afternoon.

"Abby, you're an oversexed idiot," she told herself. Even so, she scanned the crowd, looking for a wavy brown mop of hair set above a gray suit. She spied an older man in a gray track suit and decided an earlier glimpse of him from the corner of her eye must have triggered the memory. It was simply her mind playing tricks on her. Because the notion couldn't have come so easily from inside her, not in connection with . . . no.

Shading her eyes as she slipped through the chained front entrance, she scanned the bleachers for lingering guests from the last show but found no one. Even the ushers had disappeared.

Abby frowned and headed across the stage. One of the new ushers stepped out the stage door just then.

"Hey, you're not supposed—" The girl began, then halted, an uncertain smile settling on her flushed features as she recognized Abby.

"I was just getting a drink," the girl said, hurrying past. "I know. I shouldn't have left the gates unattended, but no one was around anywhere close, and I thought it would be okay for just a minute. I'm sorry, it won't happen again."

Abby hesitated, startled by the girl's vehemence.

"Okay," she said. She stared at the girl's retreating back for a moment, trying to remember her name. She'd only been there for three days and seldom spoke or called attention to herself. But she'd done her job well enough until now.

"How are the workmen doing?" Abby called after her. *Starla.* That was it. Unusual. It didn't seem to fit her wallflower attitude.

"Oh, they left hours ago," Starla replied with a vague wave of her hand. "Jay says the valve's as good as new."

"Is Jay back there now?" Abby asked suspiciously.

"Of course. Why wouldn't he be?" The fading flush returned, and Starla looked away.

Abby suppressed a knowing grin. Why not, indeed, and especially with the valve repairs finished?

Usually about this time he wandered off to the employee dining rooms, either to eat dinner or to talk with friends from the Wild West show. Sometimes he skipped the dining rooms and flirted instead with the woman who drew caricatures outside the wax museum. More than once, Abby had accused Jay of being a social firefly. He wasn't, though, not completely. He was more of a chameleon, changing just enough to fit in with whatever group he happened to be with at the time. And it appeared he was changing his colors again.

"Wonderful," Abby replied, her voice heavily laced with sarcasm. She eased the stage door closed behind her and slipped quietly down the corridor. Not that stealth was exactly necessary, with the loud calliope music drifting over from the Ferris wheel. But she wanted to catch Jay off guard, maybe shake some sense into him.

"Don't you think she's a little young for you?" she called from the top of the stairs leading down into the pit.

Jay jerked, flinging a small herring into the air as he spun around. It plopped onto the counter, then slid off the drain board into the stainless steel sink.

"Don't do that!" Jay retorted. "It's bad for my heart."

"*Your* heart isn't the one that concerns me. Like I said, she's too young for you. And too serious."

Jay stilled, then fished the herring out of the drain. "Who? Harriet Herring here? She's not my type. Besides, I'm not the fish kisser here." His playful banter sounded forced, though.

"She's a nice kid."

"Who?"

"What's her name out there, the usher," Abby gestured helplessly as the name escaped her again. "Starla."

The girl had to change her name to something more appropriate, Abby decided.

"She's nineteen," Jay said in a low voice.

"And how old are you?"

Jay shot her a dark look. "How was your appointment?"

Abby held up both hands in mock surrender. "Fine. I'll stay out of your business, you stay out of mine." She took the bucket of fish from him and picked out a handful of herring. The rest she shoved into a refrigerator. "Just one thing. Don't come crying on my shoulder if her daddy comes after you with a baseball bat."

"Her father died last year," Jay said. He faced the wall, hiding his expression. "So I guess that's one thing I won't have to worry about this time." His posture was rigid, so unlike the easygoing playboy she'd worked with for the past three years. This was serious.

"Jay?"

"She's different," he said, his expression uncertain, almost vulnerable. Then the teasing mask slid back into place. "Let me see your teeth."

Abby took a step backward.

"What?"

"Your teeth. I want to see the new one."

"I don't know how the heck that rumor got started," she said, heading for the stairs with the fish balanced in one hand. "By the way, what happened with the leak? Starla said the workmen left hours ago."

Jay let out a long, low whistle. "Whatever you said to that Gardner fellow did the trick. He had a crew from A & F Plumbing out here a half hour after you left. It took them only about an hour to locate the problem and fix it. They had a spare valve right in the truck."

"What about the park's crew?"

"Gardner sent them packing. Brett looked like he

was ready to have a cow, but he didn't say anything, at least not while they were here."

"The word is that the chairman of the board sent him down here," Abby explained. Gardner himself had hinted at that, and Bethany's grapevine had confirmed it.

Jay whistled between his teeth. "No wonder Brett's so rattled. By the way, Gardner left a note for you. I tucked it behind the edge of the phone."

Abby glanced up at the wisp of white paper showing against the bare, unfinished wall, then forced herself to look away. A show of eagerness would only give Jay more ammunition for teasing her. He had enough already.

"And the leak is completely fixed? They're not waiting on parts or anything so they can finish the job?" she asked.

"Nope."

"Drat!" The note probably named time and date for this so-called dinner she'd agreed to cook. She should have guessed before she made that rash offer that he could accomplish the impossible.

"Drat?" Jay looked at her as if she'd suddenly grown purple fur. "You're weird tonight, Abby. I thought you'd be pleased. You usually hover over Otto and Pepper like they're your own children. In fact, I'm surprised you even left this afternoon, considering everything that was going on." He watched her expectantly, as if waiting for an explanation.

Well, he could keep on waiting. Her business was hers alone, for now at least. Later, when her secret became too noticeable to hide, she'd come up with some sort of story. Or maybe she wouldn't. The truth should suffice for those she cared to tell. The rest could think what they liked.

"Okay," Jay continued, when Abby held her silence. "Sorry I asked. I just want to know one thing, though. How did you convince this guy to overrule Brett?"

Abby shrugged. "I explained the delicate chemical balance we have to maintain. And he saw how skittish Otto and Pepper were this afternoon. I blamed the leak." As she spoke, she continued up the stairs and retrieved the note with a show of nonchalance.

"That never worked before with Brett."

She halted, the note pinched between her fingers. "I never promised to cook for Brett."

Jay's eyes widened. "You're kidding, right? You bribed the guy with *your* cooking. Your corner deli potato salad is notorious."

Abby grinned. "Exactly. I shouldn't have too much trouble weaseling out of it."

"I could tell him about the time you tried to make spaghetti."

"Please do. It'll save me the trouble of bribing Bethany to do it." She tucked the note between her teeth and turned the knob with her free hand.

"So where are you going with those fish?"

"I thought I'd talk to the children a little bit, maybe play a round or two of catch with them," she said, then hesitated. "Why don't you take Starla over for a soda or something? I'll watch the gates while you're gone."

"Bribery again?"

She shook her head. "Nope. An apology. I think I may have misjudged you."

She headed down the corridor before he could answer. Alone now, she opened the note and read quickly.

I like Italian.

Abby groaned aloud. She stared at the brief message for a moment, wondering how she really could get herself out of this mess. Then she crumpled the paper and stuffed it into her pocket. She retrieved a can of tennis balls and her whistle from a nearby cabinet, then stepped out onto the stage in the empty auditorium. Two short tweets on the low-toned whistle brought Otto and Pepper to the surface of the water.

While she tossed balls to the porpoises and tried to catch those they flipped back, she watched out of the corner of her eye as Jay approached Starla. He hesitated for a moment, as if uncertain of his reception, then he spoke. Abby couldn't make out the words, but his usually jaunty tone was more subdued. The girl responded with a shy dignity, then a surprised smile. Something melted inside Abby as she watched them together, walking close but not quite touching. It brought back sweet memories of beginnings, of relationships that had since soured or faded away for one reason or another.

Without thinking, she splayed her fingers across her flat abdomen. Beginnings were always like this, exciting and wonderful, brimming with possibilities. Or they should be, she decided. Even if reality had a way of tarnishing even the most special of beginnings, there should be something worth holding in your memory. The trouble was, she had accumulated a lot of memories and no substance. *And when, Abby Monroe, did you become so cynical?* She didn't know the answer to that.

Sitting down at the pool edge, Abby let her fingers trail through the relative coolness of the water, wishing for a moment that she could trade places with Pepper. Think of it—nothing to do but cavort and play, perform a bit in return for her meals. No complicated decisions. No responsibility for choosing between unclear choices.

No freedom to choose.

She splashed the water, then touched her finger to Pepper's nose. "It's done. Or at least it's started. I'm going to be a mommy, I hope." It wasn't guaranteed, but Dr. Stephans said there was every indication she'd conceive, if not this time, then the next or the time after that. A tiny thrill surged through her at the thought. Maybe even now . . .

Never mind the uncertainty or the difficulties of single parenthood. She wanted a child. She didn't know when the wanting had started or when it had become so strong. She couldn't wait any longer for the *right* man, and any other man wouldn't be enough—not for her and not for her child. So instead, she'd chosen an anonymous donor with demonstrated intelligence and a spotless medical history. Her doctor and the clinic had made it all possible. So had Aunt Margaret's money, although Abby doubted that this is what Aunt Margaret had meant her to do with the inheritance.

Invest it in your future, Aunt Margaret had said in the letter she'd left in the safety deposit box. Only that strong-willed spinster had expected her niece to buy a house or open a business. Or maybe invest in stocks and bonds, not buy herself a procedure that would bring another life into her womb.

But just because Aunt Margaret hadn't considered it didn't mean she wouldn't approve. And in time, Pop would understand, too. Until then, she'd be satisfied with his reluctant acceptance of her choice.

Muffled footsteps distracted her. She turned away from the low wall that formed the side of the pool to see who approached.

Matt's smile caught her off guard, and she returned it without thinking. He'd changed into jeans and a loose blue T-shirt that revealed tanned, lean muscled arms.

Only the sunglasses remained, hiding his eyes and his thoughts.

"What are the ropes for?" he asked, stopping a few yards away and gesturing toward the corral-like enclosure surrounding the top of the pool. Two strands of rope were strung between tall posts around the perimeter, stopping only at the railing that separated the stage from the audience area.

"To keep the dolphins from jumping out. Last year Pepper got a little too curious and beached herself on the sidewalk over there." Abby pointed toward a section of bleachers on the far side of the pool.

"Odd. I don't think any of the other facilities do this."

"They don't have Pepper," Abby retorted, retrieving the soggy tennis balls and dropping them back into their can.

"I didn't expect to see you back here tonight." He hitched his pant leg up and propped one foot on the bleachers.

Abby shrugged. "I was worried about Otto and Pepper. What are you doing here?"

"Playing tourist."

"At least you look the part now."

He stepped back and spun around slowly, his arms spread wide. "Think I'll blend in with the crowd?"

She pretended to survey him thoughtfully. No, he looked too good to simply disappear into a sea of faces and bodies. She felt a flush rise and turned away, reaching for the bucket she'd tossed the fish into earlier. "Something's wrong," she said. "I think it's the suitcase wrinkles on your shirt."

"I thought it just looked mussed up, sort of casual." He moved closer, leaning on the waist-high wall that formed the upper edge of the pool. Only a metal railing separated them.

She braved another look at him. His sunglasses had slipped down his nose and he peered over the top of the frames at her, his expression self-assured and flirtatious. She had a sudden urge to take him down a notch or two. But then, it wasn't wise to insult the chairman's emissary.

"It's casual" was all she said.

"But not right. I don't want to stand out," he said. "It's important that I look like any other tourist while I assess the park."

"From a tourist's viewpoint," she finished for him. "Do you ride the roller coasters and everything, or just hang around with a newspaper and a notebook, trying to look unobtrusive?"

He chuckled. "Come with me and find out."

"Can't." She tweeted the whistle, calling Otto and Pepper back to the edge of the pool.

"Why not? You're off duty, aren't you?"

"Officially. But the others are gone now. I can't leave until they come back. Who knows what kind of saboteurs might be hanging around, just waiting for an opportunity to put bubble bath in the pool or feed anchovy pizzas to Otto." She softened the gibe with a wink, hoping he'd take it as lightly as she meant it. She was treading a fine line with this troubleshooter, but he appeared to have a sense of humor.

"You have a point there. Who knows? It could even have been me who broke that valve earlier."

Abby laughed. "I'd considered it. Since you didn't have any grease on your hands, I thought it unlikely."

"You actually suspected me?"

"For a minute. You were a stranger. You still are."

"That's easily changed. Come sleuthing with me tonight. I'll wait with you until the others get back. Two guards are better than one," he added when she hesitated.

"How do you know I won't tip everyone off that you're a spy from headquarters?"

"Because it's not in your best interest. Your company can't be any happier with the status quo than we are at headquarters," he said. "Am I right?"

"On target so far."

"So you'll help me out?"

"How?"

"You can be my cover. I can't just ride everything by myself. Nobody comes to an amusement park alone."

"Well," she said, drawing out the word while she considered the ramifications. It might be fun. At worst, he would turn out to be a bore, though she didn't think that was likely. And with all these people around, her virtue was certainly safe. She laid a hand across her stomach and smiled at the irony. It seemed odd to worry about the hazards of an evening with a very attractive man when only a few hours ago she'd undergone a medical procedure that replaced making love.

"I don't see why not," she said finally. "But first, we have to do something about those clothes."

"The wrinkles," he said, pulling out the tail of his shirt and glancing down.

"I'll just bet that you carry everything in one of those big garment bags, the kind with compartments for everything. And that shirt you're wearing must have been neatly folded and strapped into one of those compartments."

"So?" His brows lifted warily, as though he couldn't quite figure out where she was leading.

"So, your fold marks show," she said, touching the

offending lines on his shoulders with her free hand. Then she pointed out the crisscrossed squares at his midriff, shaking her head.

"I dressed in a hurry," he said. "And my suite doesn't come with a French maid to straighten these things out."

He caught her pointing finger before she could draw it away. The devilment glinting in his eyes sent a shiver up her arm. He drew the finger to his lips, as if to kiss it. Then in the last instant he sniffed and folded his palm around her hand.

"Fish. I should have known," he said, letting her pull her hand away.

"What did you expect? Lavender and roses?" She tweeted the whistle again, then signaled the dolphins with a quick hand motion. They circled the pool with a series of leaps, then jumped high and landed in dual splashes next to Abby and Matt. Expecting it, Abby turned her back on the wave that washed over the edge. It hit Matt full force, drenching the upper half of his body.

He stood there, motionless, his shirt pasted against his chest. Abby tossed the last of the fish to Otto and Pepper, rewarding them for their obedience to her commands. Slowly, Matt turned his head to watch her. Droplets of water trailed down his sunglasses. Finally, he removed them and wiped his forearm across his forehead. Then he shook his head, letting the water fly.

"I guess that takes care of the fold lines," he said. Slowly, his lips cracked into a grin. "You know, I was going to let you off the hook about dinner. But now, you really owe me."

"Fish all right?" she replied.

His grin widened. "I'm sure that whatever you cook will be fine. Although I am partial to Italian."

"I got the note."

"I wasn't sure."

Abby nodded, then saw with relief that Jay and Starla had returned. The two of them waved a greeting, then set to work readying the arena for the next show. Abby pitched in, more to escape Matt's taunting gaze than because she thought they needed her help. He'd taken her prank well. He'd practically begged for it, she told herself. Still, his cheerful mien made her nervous. Something else was there behind the grin, something measuring, a depth she hadn't anticipated. Or maybe she was just prone to nervousness today. Yes, that was it.

"What happened to you two?" Jay asked as he passed them, winding up the rope that was strung around the edge of the pool between shows.

"Don't ask," Abby whispered, not wanting to explain. She was beginning to feel embarrassed. She'd been childish to pull that prank on him. Surely a thirty-three-year-old veteran of the dating arena could come up with a better set-down than that.

"She fixed my shirt," Matt said glibly, then took her arm, tugging her toward the exit. "Now if you don't need her any more this evening, I'm kidnapping her. Have fun, kids, and don't forget to lock up."

"Abby?" Jay looked startled.

"I have my keys" was all she could manage. Following Matt's lead, she hopped over the chain and hurried around the corner past the Snow Cone stand and into the revelrous New Orleans corridor.

They dodged a cluster of carousing teenagers, then ducked behind a hamburger stand. "Sorry, I forgot to ask if you had a jacket or something you wanted to bring with you."

Abby pulled her hand away and straightened her

shirt, pulling the clinging wetness off her back. "I'd like to pick up my purse sometime before Jay locks up, but other than that, no. What's first?"

"Let's start here, then work our way around the circle. Which way?" He pointed to the fork in the wide paved pathway they'd just left.

"To the right. I want to save Appalachia for last."

"Why?"

"You haven't lived until you've ridden the Mountain Mine Cars at night," she replied.

The path arced back into the California Shores section. Their first stop was the Octopus.

"You didn't just eat, did you?" he said as they made their way through the maze of iron rails designed to keep the waiting lines orderly and compact.

"Don't worry, these things don't bother me a bit. I have a cast-iron stomach," she told him, stepping into place behind a grandmotherly type with two shoulder-high girls. She quickly counted the people ahead of them and smiled. "We shouldn't have to wait more than five minutes."

"I'd say closer to ten," he argued. "The attendant's moving in slow motion."

Abby leaned back against the rail. She had to agree. The kid was moving slower than usual. Or maybe she'd just never noticed before. "Is that going down in your little notebook? Or do you carry a voice-activated tape recorder?"

"My notebook is probably as soaked as the rest of me," he replied. "I'm more interested in overall impressions just now anyway. I'll work on the specifics later."

"That makes sense," Abby said, glancing around her. Overall, this place appeared well used, maybe even a little run-down. The paint was more chipped than present on the rails here. And a spiderweb of cracks covered the asphalt paths nearby and underneath the Octopus itself.

"So tell me about your job," he prompted.

She smiled. "There's not much to it. I work five days a week, including weekends. Some days I do all seven shows. Some days I split them with Jay. We also clean the filters, test the chemical mix, stuff like that. We usually take time to work on new routines with Otto and Pepper. We can't do too much, though, or they'll be too full at show time."

"From the fish rewards," he surmised.

"That's right. A kind word and a pat on the beak don't work nearly as well as a nice fat cod. And we have to be consistent with the rewards, or they won't cooperate. And then, there are days like today, when nothing seems to work anyway."

"You put in a lot of hours then."

Abby nodded and moved up as the line shifted. "I'm used to it. What else do I have to do with my time anyway? If I were home, Pop would just con me into mowing the lawn or cleaning the bathroom."

"He could always toss you a fish."

"Chocolate would work much better," she replied with a grin, then moved forward. She turned to speak again, then noticed his attention was centered somewhere to the right. She followed the direction of his gaze to the Model T course.

"It's always quiet over there, though usually not this bad," she commented.

"What else is slow?" he asked.

Abby considered. "Brett should have figures on that from the turnstile counters at all the attractions."

"Sometimes the numbers are misleading. Which ride always has a line and which has lots of empty seats?"

"I'm not sure. People don't talk much about the ones they think are duds. I don't see too many people on the Ski Lift, but then there was that accident back East last year, so I suppose people are a little leery." She spent the next few minutes repeating what she'd overheard about the supposedly good rides. And then it was their turn to climb aboard the cramped, twirling car.

Or at least it seemed cramped when he squeezed his frame in next to hers and she tried to sit without touching him. Somehow, he seemed larger than he had before. Or maybe it was just that he was bigger than Bethany or Maureen's two kids combined.

Her stomach lurched, then settled, as their arm of the ride lifted and the car spun. Five seconds later, she gave up the struggle to keep from touching him and let the force of the car's movement throw her against him. She could feel his muscles bunch and clench as he shifted, then slid his arm around her. Abby stiffened unconsciously.

"Careful, you'll blow my cover," he shouted over the noise of the ride.

He'd noticed. Abby told herself to relax. Her body was just beginning to obey when the loud whir of the engine ceased, and they coasted to a halt.

"Hey, you're the dolphin lady!" the attendant said as he unlatched the door to their car. "I didn't recognize you before."

"That's me," Abby replied, waving to the kid as she followed Matt out. "So much for your cover," she added more quietly once they passed through the counter gate.

"No problem. I'll just pretend to be your date. Nobody'll suspect anything else." He took her hand and pulled her closer.

"What are you doing?" she asked, startled.

"Don't couples in amusement parks hold hands?" He glanced around him, then pointed. "See? Over there. There's one, two, no, three couples that I can see right now."

Abby smiled sweetly. "Fine. But that's the hand I held the fish in."

His fingers tightened around hers, then released them. "You're such a flirt. Wait here. I'll be right back." He disappeared around the corner of the Octopus hut.

Abby waited five minutes, then ten, or so it seemed without a watch to check. Then she noticed a commotion on the other side of the hut. A few seconds later, Matt reappeared, escorted by a security officer she recognized.

"Sorry, sir. I didn't realize who you were," the man was saying.

"That's all right. It's good to know that you security people are on top of things," Matt replied, then shook hands briefly with him.

"What was that all about?" Abby asked when the officer was gone.

Matt led her down the pathway toward the next ride while he spoke. "I was just checking the maintenance records. I heard an odd squeak mixed in with the normal engine sounds."

"A squeak? You picked that out of all that noise?" Abby looked at him in surprise. He seemed distracted, as if puzzling out the source of the sound. Either he was putting on a heck of a bluff, or he was even more astute than she'd guessed. She suspected the latter was true.

They followed the same routine through the next three rides, although Matt took greater care not to get caught snooping. It wasn't until they were settled in a booth, sipping soft drinks, that his attention returned completely to her. He'd just spent a couple of minutes jotting in a tiny notebook, then suddenly he glanced up.

"Your eyes," he said. "I can't decide what color they are."

"Gray." Maybe he was color-blind.

"They look green now."

Abby glanced down at the green tabletop, then around at the green walls. "It's just a trick of the light."

"When we were in that yellow car, on that flying thing, they had flecks of gold." He tucked the notebook into a back pocket, never taking his eyes from hers. The sunglasses were gone now, lost someplace between the Octopus and the Flying Wright Planes.

"My driver's license says gray," she said, trying to ignore the seduction in his voice. It wasn't intentional, she was sure. Until this moment, he'd seemed more concerned with the shortcomings of the park than with her. And she wasn't sure she wanted that to change. She didn't want his voice to purr along her nerve endings or ignite thoughts that were better left to those more intimately acquainted. But the press of his body against hers during the frantic, exhilarating spins and twists of the rides had stirred up those blasted hormones again.

"Your sister said you used to be an actress."

Abby shrugged. "I have a B.S. in theater and an unimpressive list of credits in dinner theater. It was enough to get me the job with Marine Shows, though. They look for people with showmanship and no previous experience. We don't have bad training habits and we work cheap."

"Do you share an apartment with your sister? Or

do you live alone?" he asked, abruptly changing the subject.

She hesitated. What exactly was he asking?

"Both of us still live at home with Pop," she said.

"Really?"

"It's cheaper," Abby replied. "And more convenient for me than a sublet or some horribly furnished condo like the one the company provides for Jay. And during the winter, when we move Pepper and Otto to Tulsa, I stay with my cousin. Pretty parochial, huh?"

A shadow crossed his expression. "Sounds nice. I travel so much that I don't get to spend much time with my family."

"Tell me about them."

He shrugged. "There's just my mother and father now and a couple of aunts and cousins I haven't seen since I was twelve."

"You're an only child?" Abby couldn't imagine growing up alone.

"I had a sister once. She died."

"I'm sorry."

He took her hand. "It was a long time ago. Come on, it's almost dark now. What do you say we head over to the Mine Cars?"

Abby stood up, letting him lead her back outside. "Not dark enough yet. But there's a few things to check out between here and there."

They played bumper cars, then challenged one another to foosball. Abby won, though barely. And she suspected he'd have beaten her soundly if he wasn't playing the troubleshooter at the same time. By the time they reached the Sawmill Chute at the edge of the Appalachia section, late dusk had deepened to night, and the stars were popping out overhead.

"Time for the Mountain Mine Cars," Abby said.

"This first," he said, nudging her toward the water ride. "I love these things."

"And you've already been christened today," she replied, laughing. She was enjoying this more than she'd expected. It was what she'd needed to shake off the restlessness of this afternoon. A little fun. A little human warmth.

She told him more about her family while they waited in line, responding to his questions easily until he asked about her social life, specifically her dating habits.

"I just want to know whether I might have to deal with a jealous football player before the night's over," he teased.

"No football players," she answered, avoiding the real question. He wouldn't let the subject drop, though.

"Any other professions?"

"I'm not seeing anyone just now."

"Good. Because I'd like to see more of you."

"You still have a home-cooked dinner to collect," she reminded him. Heaven knows what she'd cook— or burn. But she wouldn't mind testing his sense of humor a bit more. She wouldn't mind spending more time with him, so long as she managed to keep her perspective. He was in town for only a short time after all.

"Tomorrow?"

"A long day," she said. "It's Jay's day off."

"Then when?"

"Don't you have a full schedule?"

"I have to eat sometimes. And your house is close."

Abby regarded him suspiciously. "How did you know?"

"You said it was convenient. And I looked in your personnel record," he confessed.

She stiffened. "I'm not sure I like that."

"I didn't single you out. I skimmed through a whole stack of key files today. Yours was just more interesting since we had such a memorable meeting. We're next," he continued, switching subjects without a change in tone.

It took Abby a moment to absorb what he'd said last, she was so distracted by his confession. She hadn't thought about the personnel file. All medical claims had to be filed through the personnel office. Since the fertility treatments weren't covered, she hadn't filed any claims for them. But there were other records, earlier records that she'd rather he didn't see.

Then she noticed the red-haired teenager flirting openly with Matt. Abby frowned and stepped quickly into the waiting seat. The redhead and her giggling companion slipped into the rear compartment. Apparently, they'd all be sharing a boat.

"Wait a minute," the redhead called before Matt could settle into the spot directly behind Abby. "Can we trade? I'd rather sit up front."

"Sorry, maybe next time," he replied, then straddled the padded bench and pulled Abby up against him. "The little flirt should be locked up for her own protection," he whispered in Abby's ear.

Abby giggled and leaned forward. "She's half your age, Pops."

"And I'm so ancient? How old are you, Grandma?"

"You read my file," she reminded him as they leaned into the first curve. The boat eased around it, barely bumping the side of the raised trough that carried them through the thin stand of woods toward the big hill. Two curves later, their boat thumped into the one ahead, throwing Matt hard against Abby. He groaned, then slid back on the seat, pulling her with him.

"Having fun?" he said so close to her ear she could feel the warmth of his breath.

"Yeah. Taking notes?"

"Not right now. I need both hands for this."

"What a line," Abby retorted. But she didn't move away. She wanted to pretend for a while longer that she had someone special to share things with, even if logic told her that Matt wasn't a likely candidate for any long-term sharing. She still had a little time to enjoy herself before she had to toe the line. So long as she observed certain boundaries, she wasn't endangering the future she'd planned.

Finally, their boat nosed onto the treadmill that took them up the hill. And when the nose tipped over the top, Abby leaned forward, ready to duck below the prow to avoid the splash at the bottom. Matt pulled her back. The water hit her full in the face, drenching her, drenching them both.

"You guys are wet," the redhead commented as their boat coasted toward the exit ramp.

"Really wet," Matt agreed, slicking his hair back from his face while he watched Abby wipe the water from her eyes. "And now we're even."

Abby grimaced and faced forward again, pulling the clinging shirt away from her body. She suspected she looked like a candidate for a wet T-shirt contest.

"Are you angry?"

Abby glanced over her shoulder. He looked worried. "Of course not. I expected to get somewhat wet on this ride. Not this wet but splashed a bit. I'd be a rotten sport if I let something like this bother me, especially after what I did to you."

He squeezed her shoulder in response, then clambered out as they reached the exit. He helped Abby, keeping hold of her hand. They were nearly out of the Sawmill Chute complex when he tugged her behind a small building.

"You're full of surprises," she said, staring up at him. Even though they were hidden from sight, they were only a few feet from the other departing Chute fans. An overhead street light shone brightly, illuminating the concern in his expression.

"Sure you aren't mad?" he asked.

She shook her head, unable to tear her eyes from his. She swayed closer, or maybe he moved. She didn't care.

Then the bushes parted.

"Oops, sorry," a young voice quipped, then giggled. "Sorry, babe, this spot's taken." The screen of branches sprang closed, but the moment was lost.

Abby smiled ruefully up at Matt, but he was staring in irritation at the bush. "Come on," she said, tugging him back onto the path. "It's dark enough for the Mine Cars now."

The line was long when they reached the roller coaster, but Abby insisted it was worth the wait. "You'll love it," she said. "Believe me, it's not what you're expecting."

Matt wasn't convinced. "I've ridden everything Amusements America owns, including this roller coaster."

"But I'll bet you haven't ridden this one in the dark," she said. "Just wait. You'll see."

Finally, it was their turn to climb into a car in the short train. "Watch the lights so you'll know where we're going," she said, straddling the bench once again. The ride was so tame and smooth that it didn't require shoulder restraints. She leaned back against Matt, pretending to relax. But she could barely contain her glee. Somehow she didn't think this high-level executive had time to read the fine print on the operation of all the rides.

When they hit the first dip, Matt leaned left in anticipation of the curve the lights marked. Abby laughed as the car dropped low into a dark, unlit hollow, following the track in the opposite direction. That was the fun of the Mine Cars after dark, the surprises brought on by the deceptive lights that made the tourists think they'd go one way, when the cars really went another.

"You lied," he yelled.

"I know," she shouted back while she braced for the next turn. Sixty seconds later, the train of cars rolled back into the covered building and braked to a stop.

Abby leaped to the walkway ahead of Matt, then practically danced out into the night air. "Tricked you, huh? That's the fun of it," she taunted, still high from the exhilaration of the ride.

"I admit it. You were right," he said. He finger-combed his hair, then gave up. "I guess the disguise is complete."

Abby pretended to survey him critically. "Well, compared with this afternoon, I'd say it's a pretty drastic change."

"Good. I'm thirsty again."

"Me, too. We're close to the employee snack bar," she said, turning him away from the drink stand. "Stuff's cheaper there."

"I'm buying," he argued.

"It's your money," she said but kept walking. When they turned the corner and stepped beyond the barriers, Matt picked up his speed beside her. Then he disappeared.

Abby halted, glancing around her. Where had his investigating nose led him this time? A hand shot out from behind a freestanding section of fence. She had only a quick glimpse of Matt's face before he pulled her behind the fence with him.

She landed hard against his chest. Strong hands caught her shoulders and held her there for a moment. Abby drew a great shuddering breath, then stilled. Her knees trembled as rough denim brushed against her sensitive skin.

Then his hands feathered against her face, turning her chin upward, making it impossible to look away. His lips touched hers in the briefest of caresses. She gasped at the feel of it, at the sparks that shot through her. Then she stretched closer, deepening the kiss, savoring the feel of him, the flavor of him.

This, she thought, *this is what had been missing all day*. She needed this warmth, this touch of passion. It chased away the feel of the cold clinic table against her back, the chill of the impersonal, almost humiliating examination and subsequent procedure. It brought the right emotions back into her heart.

Then Matt lifted his head, and reality intruded once more. *Keep it in perspective*, she reminded herself. It was just a kiss, born of starlight, shared fun, and her own confused emotions. She'd probably sent out all sorts of crazy signals tonight.

He cupped her cheek in his palm, caressing her throat with his thumb. Abby swallowed. Then he kissed her once more, slowly, lingering until they were both breathless.

This time, when he drew back, he looked as startled as she felt. It wasn't hormones, she realized. These feelings were real, a powerful blend of chemistry that picked the most unlikely time and place to erupt. Chemistry with an improper stranger.

"Is this going to be in your report?" she asked shakily, struggling for lightness.

His lips touched her forehead, then he pressed her tightly against him, holding her close. "No, this is just you and me," he whispered.

FOUR

Abby Monroe was full of surprises. Watching her show this afternoon, Matt had been taken with her poise and sense of humor, not to mention the way her well-shaped legs flexed with every step. She was good, damn good. And intriguing. She'd told him very little about herself, letting him only so close, then deflecting his questions. The lady kept her secrets. But that only made her more interesting.

Tonight, though, he'd touched hidden fire, tasted it. And he wanted more. Even now, an hour after he'd tucked her into her father's station wagon, he couldn't concentrate on the printouts scattered across the conference room table in front of him. The columns of numbers simply couldn't compete with the memory of her lips moving against his, of her small, firm body in his arms. He wished she'd stayed there longer instead of pulling away, her eyes uncertain and her hands shaking.

He couldn't afford to think about that now. He had work to do. The CEO expected answers. The board of directors wanted to know whether funds were being embezzled or the park was just grossly mismanaged. But instead of studying the evidence, he found himself wondering what secrets hid behind Abby's dove-gray eyes. He wondered whether she was as distracted as he.

He picked up the telephone and dialed the number in the file in front of him. Abby answered on the first ring, her voice low and distracted.

"I wanted to make sure you got home safely. I won't keep you up," he said reluctantly. He found he needed to hear her voice for a little while.

"It's all right. I was reading," she replied.

"Reading what?" He wanted to hear her voice for a little longer.

"*The Secret Language of Dolphins*."

"Trying to find a new way to reach Otto?"

She laughed, the rich, vibrant sound reminding him of the passion in her kiss. "Not exactly. A friend gave it to me for my birthday. It's been sitting around, gathering dust."

"What made you pick it up tonight?"

She didn't answer for a moment. "I was too wound up to sleep when I got home. I guess it was the roller coasters."

Matt smiled. He didn't think so. At least he hoped it wasn't the roller coasters that kept the adrenaline flowing strongly enough to keep her awake into the night. "You sound as if you've calmed down," he said.

"I've just put things into perspective."

"Meaning?"

"Tonight was fun," she said lightly.

"I thought it was more than fun. I'd call it a promising beginning." He couldn't remember when a simple kiss had shaken him like that. And he couldn't put it out of his mind.

"You're not going to be here long. That means you're not my type." Threads of steel laced through her teasing tone.

"Maybe you'll give me a chance to change your mind," he suggested.

"I'll pay up and fix you dinner. That's all. I'm getting too old for games."

Too old? What did that make him? "Maybe you just haven't learned to play the game. Maybe the rules always scared you away."

"Some things aren't meant to be played at. I'm thirty-three years old. I've been married and divorced. I know how to play," she said, sounding sad. "I choose not to. That way nobody gets hurt."

He drew a deep breath. "Why don't we just keep it light, not take things so seriously?"

"Maybe we should forget about dinner," she suggested uncertainly.

"Why? You have to eat. I have to eat, and I'm tired of restaurant food and hot dog stands."

"Tomorrow night, then," she said.

"Right. What are we having?"

"I'm not sure yet," she said, a hint of laughter stealing back into her voice.

Matt smiled as he replaced the receiver. He really didn't have time for this. But she was a fresh change from the sleek, sophisticated matchsticks he'd dated lately. Abby Monroe had substance and a history she'd only hinted at. He wondered what drove her. Earlier tonight, she'd seemed open and friendly, sometimes painfully blunt. Yet when his questions became personal, an invisible wall rose around her. He frowned, remembering how she'd reacted when he'd jokingly mentioned getting her address from her personnel file. She'd turned white as the walls of this room.

He fished her file out of the stack of papers at the end of the table and flipped through it again. He paused a moment, staring at the small park I.D. photo. It didn't do her justice. She was much more attractive, beautiful in an athletic sort of way. He skimmed through the rest of the file. As before, he found nothing that would explain her sudden pallor. With anyone else, he'd blame it on nerves. Not Abby, though. She certainly hadn't been intimidated by him personally.

He ran through the pages, more slowly this time. He began to see a pattern, though he wasn't sure what it meant. A note from Brett Holland citing her for excessive absences in March and April. An unusual number of insurance claims during that period. Then the claims ended. There were none for June or July. That didn't mean anything, though, except that she'd been sick. It could have been no more than a chronic ear infection. Big deal. The only other item out of the ordinary seemed to be a citation for insubordination, again from Brett Holland, though no specifics were mentioned.

Matt shoved the conference room chair back and stretched, trying to shake off his restless thoughts. Then he returned his attention to the printouts. His instincts told him he was missing a connection somewhere. He took out the personnel files again, not just hers, but those of all the key employees. After a couple of hours, the pattern became clear. Missing money. Citations for insubordination, all signed by Brett Holland. The man had one hand in the till and the other in an iron grip around potential whistle-blowers, Matt surmised.

"That's it," he muttered, reaching for the phone again. Slowly, he dialed the private number of the CEO of Amusements America, Inc. It took only a few minutes to relay his suspicions, but it would take days to prove them. Meanwhile, any private dinners, any private time at all, would be out of the question. Otherwise, he might fail to contain the damage. Then heads would roll off the chopping block, with his own at the lead.

But maybe, just maybe, he could spare an hour or two for a certain strong-willed blonde. After all, he had to eat.

The following morning, Abby decided the man made sense. Why take this flirtation so seriously? Matt Gardner was fun, and fun was what she needed to take her mind off matters she couldn't control.

Bethany wasn't so sure. "I can't believe you're dating the man," her sister said as she guided her subcompact through the Thursday morning traffic. "You do like living on the edge, don't you? First this baby thing, now late nights on the roller coaster with the Hatchet Man."

Abby hesitated, throwing her sister a sharp look. "Hatchet Man? Is that what they're calling him?"

"Behind his back. The word is that when Matt Gardner shows up, somebody's head ends up on the chopping block. I want to be sure it isn't mine."

"Brett's the one who should be worried," Abby reminded her. "You're only the personnel director. You just follow orders."

Bethany sighed, glancing over at Abby as she eased the car to a stop at a traffic light. "I'm part of the management team, and we both know the park hasn't been doing well. We'll be lucky if Gardner doesn't close the place down and fire us all. If that happens, Marine Shows will transfer you out of Kansas City, so you'd better be watching out for your job, too."

"At least I wouldn't have you nagging at me," Abby retorted lightly, then changed the subject.

Half an hour later, she was on her way through the south entrance, waiting impatiently in the line of workers clocking in. She spotted Matt out of the corner of her eye, coming out the double doors of the administration building. A stubble growth of beard shadowed his chin. His shirt was rumpled and limp. He saw her and changed direction, the beginnings of a tired smile on his lips.

"Have you decided yet?" he asked.

She stepped out of line, turning her back on the curious stares of the other employees. "Nope. I'll decide at the store. You'll just have to be surprised," she said.

"It's been nothing but surprises so far," he replied. A spark flared in his dark eyes, touching off an answering flame that burned past her guard. This man could be dangerous, she decided, if she wasn't careful. But if anything, Abby was careful. She'd learned she had to be.

"You look tired," she said.

He rubbed his bristled chin. "Thank you for not saying I look as if I slept in my clothes. I didn't, you know."

She nodded. "You didn't sleep at all, I'd bet. I hope it was worth it."

"It might be," he said, pulling back into himself.

That was as much as she'd get out of him, she decided. "We could postpone dinner if you want to make an early night of it."

"That won't be necessary. I'm on my way to the hotel now. I'll catch a few winks before my noon meeting."

"Don't let me keep you," she said, backing away and rejoining the line.

"Yes, I do need to be going," he said. His eyes

dropped lower, surveying her clothing. "You're out of uniform. I like it though. I think the pinks will match."

"Excuse me?"

"You'll see." He waved and turned toward the parking lot. Abby watched him a long moment, wondering what she'd let herself in for. He seemed too good to be true. Then someone bumped her from behind.

"Come on, you're holdin' up the line," grumbled a teenager with a bad case of acne and an even worse attitude.

Abby glared coolly at the boy. "I don't need this. It's damned ridiculous," she muttered. She stepped out of line and hurried through the gates, holding up her pass to the security guards watching the entrance. Forget the time clock and Brett's silly policies.

By the time she arrived at the pit, she was ten minutes later than usual. She hurriedly unlocked the door and skipped down the stairs, only to come to a dead stop at the bottom. A half-dozen roses in varying shades of pink rested in a plastic cup atop the small freezer. She sniffed the blooms, breathing in the perfume of the soft petals. Strange. Who had put them here?

She buried her nose in the petals again. Matt had done it. This is what he meant by that parting remark about matching pinks. The dew-damp petals spread above short, roughly cut stems that appeared suspiciously as though they'd been swiped from one of the park's flower beds. A wave of warm, fuzzy emotion filled her. Somehow, these flowers meant more than a tissue-paper package of long-stemmed beauties from the florist.

She called the administration building and left a brief message with Brett's secretary, knowing she would pass it on to Matt. "Thanks" was all she said. The administrative staff would think she meant the repair job at the pool. Matt would know better.

She half expected to find him again in the audience or down in the pit between shows. But by three o'clock, she decided she was being silly. The man had his own work to do, so she slipped away for a late lunch.

She should have stayed. When she returned to the pit, she found a note tucked above the telephone. *Chinese is good, too,* it said. The handwriting matched that on the note Matt had left yesterday.

"Jay," she called down the stairs. "Who left this?"

"The man himself. He only had a minute, so he didn't wait. He said to tell you he'd catch you later." Her partner wore a wide grin. "Never thought I'd see the day you started kissing up to the brass."

"In your ear," she retorted. She grabbed her whistle and headed for the pool. An hour later, a messenger delivered another note in a sealed envelope. *Sorry. Unavoidable meeting at six tonight. I'll call about dinner when I know what's happening.*

Three days passed without a word from him, though a fresh set of flowers appeared in the cup each morning. No note, no calls, just the flowers. Bethany, however, had her doubts about the source.

"It couldn't be him," Bethany insisted on the ride into work on Monday morning. "It's too sentimental for somebody like him and too much trouble. He'd have a florist deliver them. Are you sure it isn't Jay? You know what a flirt he is."

Abby snorted. "Not a chance. I'm telling you, these flowers were fresh-picked. Twice they still had dew on the petals. Jay doesn't even wake up before noon, even when he's at work."

"Believe me. It couldn't be Matt Gardner," Bethany insisted. "If he doesn't have time for a phone call, he doesn't have time to pick flowers and sneak them into a locked room. You must have another secret admirer."

As much as she tried to forget them, Bethany's words kept ringing through Abby's mind, tarnishing her pleasure over the fresh bunch of gladiolus blossoms she found when she reached the pit that morning. She moved the flowers aside and began weighing out the two pounds of thawed fish she'd need for the first show of the day. But the soft peach blossoms drew her gaze, reminding her of the man who'd left them there.

The man she thought had left them there. Maybe she was only kidding herself. Why would a corporate bigwig go to the trouble of picking flowers himself, especially when he hadn't even acknowledged her phone calls to thank him? His kiss had curled her toes, but there was no reason to think it affected him the same way. No reason except her own intuition and the bemused look in his eyes as he held her. She wasn't sure either could be trusted.

"Hey, Abby," Jay called from the top of the stairs, startling her out of her reverie. "Maybe I should try the flower routine. It sure got your attention."

Abby guiltily turned back to the scale. "I don't know what you're talking about," she lied.

"Right. Don't kid a kidder, as your father always says." He skipped down the steps, whistling a jaunty tune. He opened the chemical cabinet and began testing the chemical mix in the pool water.

She forgot about the fish bucket. "What are you doing here?"

"Nothing much. I just thought I'd come in and help you out this morning." When she didn't answer, he threw up his hands in surrender, meeting her suspicious glare with a mischievous wink. "I'm having breakfast with Starla in the east dining hall," he confessed.

"I see," Abby answered, dragging the words out as she watched him. "Does Starla know? Or were you planning to waylay her when she gets to work again?"

"She invited me," he said with a hint of triumph in his voice. "I think she might like me a little."

"Just a bit," Abby replied with a sidelong glance in his direction. That was the understatement of the year, she decided, remembering how they'd been together a few days ago. Something serious must be happening between them to put Jay in such a good mood before breakfast.

"Have you found out who your secret admirer is?" he asked, stepping up behind her. He'd discounted Matt Gardner as the source two days ago when the offering had consisted of a handful of giant marigolds. The pungent scent of that bouquet had competed in strength with the thawing fish, nearly driving the entire staff out of the pit. Jay was laying odds on the maintenance supervisor.

He lifted a long stalk of blossoms from the plastic cup to tickle her under the chin with the soft tip. "We could stake the place out early tomorrow, see if we can catch the guy in the act."

Abby snatched the stalk away and put it back into the makeshift vase. "I'm not sure I want to know. I don't want to be disillusioned. It might turn out to be some chubby, bald gardener."

"A gardener wouldn't have brought you those smelly yellow things you got the other day."

"Maybe we're missing something here," she suggested. "The flowers might be for you. A certain artist could be jealous of all the attention you're paying to Starla."

Jay shook his head, a twinkle lighting his eyes. "She doesn't have a passkey. Neither do any of the gardeners."

Abby gathered up her keys and started up the stairs. "I'll walk you out."

"Come on and eat with us. You can be the chaperone."

"That's not my idea of a good time," she retorted. "Besides, I think I'll check out the maintenance man theory. I need to pick up some disinfectant. The vet called this morning. The samples we sent him had mold spores in them."

"You're kidding!"

She shook her head. "We must have picked them up when we opened the curette package. Now I keep smelling mildew. It's probably in my head, but I think we'd better scrub the place down again just in case. Don't you think so?"

"That's maintenance's job," Jay said.

"When do you think they'll ever get around to it?"

"That's something you ought to take up with your friend in the suit."

"Sorry. I haven't seen him for days."

"Right," Jay said, sounding unconvinced. "I'll help you scrub down after breakfast. Right now, I'd better run. Can't keep the lady waiting. You understand, don't you?" He smiled broadly, then flipped on the noisy filter and headed up the stairs before she could protest, not that she had anything to complain about. His shift didn't start for four hours yet anyway.

She watched as he whistled his way out the door and up the path. A moment later, she took off in the opposite direction, making her way to the maintenance warehouse on the west side of the park. The sun dipped behind a cloud as she left the main pathway. She hopped over a gate and followed the paved road behind the trees to the metal building. A delivery truck was leaving as she rounded the corner. She sidestepped off the roadway into the soft grass.

No one was around in the offices, so she went straight back into the warehouse. She'd just get what she needed and leave a note at the secretary's desk. If somebody didn't like it, they could talk to Brett about it. It wouldn't be the first time she'd crossed swords over the issue of maintenance.

She found the disinfectant high on a shelf beyond her reach. She located a six-foot stepladder over by the loading bay. It was no bigger than the one she'd used last summer when she repainted the ceilings in Dad's house. But it was awkward to maneuver between the aisles of shelving. She'd just come around a particularly difficult corner when starched white cotton framed by pin-striped lapels filled her vision. She backed away and gazed up into Matt's startled face.

"You?" she squeaked, startled by his sudden appearance in such an unlikely place. "What are you doing here?"

"Inventory," he said. "What are you doing?"

"Robbing the inventory. Want to help me with this ladder?"

He didn't move for a moment. He just stood there, watching her with a stupefied expression. Then he shrugged his shoulders in a careless gesture and handed her his clipboard. "Why not? What are you looking for?"

"Disinfectant. Top shelf at the end of the aisle."

"Your wish is my command." He took the ladder from her, manipulating it easily in the cramped quarters. "What do you want it for? Didn't you put in a requisition form?"

"Two weeks ago. They sent only half what we needed, so we're out already."

"Submit another requisition. I know it's inconvenient, but it helps keep the inventory straight." He turned thoughtful eyes on her for an instant. ''Is this even your job?''

''Maintenance is supposed to wash down the place with disinfectant twice a week.''

''If you keep on doing it, they'll assume they don't have to bother,'' he said. ''Division of labor doesn't work if you keep doing your job and somebody else's as well. If maintenance won't do the job right, report them.''

Abby snorted. ''What do I tell the mildew in the meantime? Slow down the growth, boys?''

Matt steadied the ladder, then stood it upright, clamping the spreaders into place and positioning it so all four legs rested evenly on the floor. ''I take it you've had this trouble before,'' he said.

She shot him an irritated look and scampered up the ladder. ''Sometimes it's easier to do it yourself than to keep bucking the system,'' she said. She handed him down a gallon jug, then hesitated. ''Maybe I should stock up.''

He squinted up at her. ''Maybe you should see if the system changes in the next couple of weeks.''

An uneasy feeling stole into the pit of her stomach. ''Could you be a little more specific?''

''Not until it's official.''

''You're closing the park,'' she accused, sinking into a seated position at the top of the ladder. *No. Not now when everything else is going according to plan.* The silent scream of frustration stuck in her throat as she stared at the neatly labeled bottles lining the shelf opposite her.

Matt's sigh punctuated her own. ''I'm ordering some changes. I can't say what yet, not until the chairman of the board gets here. It's up to him to make the announcement.''

"When will that be?"

He pursed his lips as he glanced down at his watch. "In about two hours. By the way, I'll need a formal statement from you and Ray."

"Jay," she corrected.

"Right. The other dolphin trainer. Okay if I stop by the dolphin pool between shows this evening?"

"Are you bringing the chairman?"

"If he wants to come."

Abby drew a deep breath. "I guess I'll have to have a little talk with Otto about his behavior. I can't have him playing hooky in front of the chairman."

She stood up, wobbling the ladder with her sudden movement. Matt grabbed it to steady it. "Be careful," he grated out as he took the two additional gallon jugs she handed down. "By the way, this stuff is concentrated. You don't use it straight."

"I know. It takes a lot to scrub down the pit."

"That isn't your responsibility," he repeated. "Let these guys earn their pay."

"The health of the dolphins is my responsibility, as are my own sinuses. I can't afford to wait for the maintenance staff to get around to my mildew problem. Besides, you saw what happened with the leak."

She handed him the last jug. "That should be enough for the next week at least," she said, starting down the ladder. When he didn't move away, she hesitated, then stepped down two more rungs. She stopped near the bottom, enclosed in the circle of his arms. Standing close enough to feel the radiating warmth of his body against her bare arms and legs, she waited for him to move.

"Excuse me, please," she murmured. His brows lifted in a subtle question, but he didn't move away.

He reminded her of a cat watching his prey, waiting with deceptive disinterest.

"Are you in a hurry?" He tipped his watch up. "You don't have a show for another hour."

"Memorizing all the schedules?"

"Only the important ones. Do you have to be somewhere right away?"

"I have a little time," Abby admitted. "You wanted to talk about something?" She leaned back against the ladder, away from the heat of his body.

"Yes, I do," he said. "I was looking forward to dinner the other night. I'm sorry business interfered."

Food wasn't what she was thinking of, and she knew he wasn't either. Her mouth went dry as his lips moved, and she remembered how they'd felt against her own lips. The spark of interest in his eyes had intensified to bonfire proportions. Though he made no move to touch her, she felt drawn toward him like the proverbial moth to the flame. And the knowledge lit tiny fires of need within her.

It felt good to need and be needed. But that's all there was between them. Physical need. Nothing to sneeze at, but not enough to act on either, not at this point in her life.

She shuttered her gaze as she carefully chose her words. "I like you, probably too much for my own good," she admitted. "But I'm not a little toy you can play around with whenever there's time and opportunity."

"You deserve better than that," he finished for her.

Her gaze narrowed suspiciously. "Don't patronize me."

"Then don't judge me until you know me," he replied. He leaned closer, letting his voice drop to a husky whisper. "I outgrew toys years ago."

His eyes, so close and so dark, revealed nothing of

his thoughts. His lips, when they touched hers, teased open the shutters she'd so carefully closed over her feelings. Honeyed sweetness poured through her with the intensity of a first love. Only this wasn't innocent and naive. It was full-bodied and mature, an emotion born of the ripeness of time and place. She wondered if he felt it, too, or if it was only her hormones and wishful thoughts playing tricks on her again.

Her fingers followed the lines of his lapel to the soft curling hairs at his collar. She linked her fingers behind his head, pulling him closer, deeper into the kiss. And she returned it with everything she was feeling. No games. No pretense. Just honest emotions all tangled into a seething pool of building desire.

A loud banging from the cargo bay jolted Abby to her senses. An earthy expletive, followed by a loud crash, shattered the last tendrils of the sensual spell. Then the cargo door clattered open. Although they were hidden from immediate view, she knew they could be discovered at any moment. She broke the kiss and leaned back, giggling softly. "I feel like a teenager caught fooling around in the library, except our librarian never used those words."

"I never got kissed like that when I was a teenager," Matt answered, winking. "I like being grown up." He captured her hands before she could pull away.

Her fingers curled around his, trembling slightly. "Is that so?"

"Absolutely. Dodge ball was never this much fun."

A box thumped to the floor at the end of the aisle. "Hey, buddy," an older man in a grease-stained blue uniform called. "Take your girlfriend somewhere else. This place is off-limits to tourists."

"Caught again," she muttered with a low giggle.

"Come on, move along now. This is a hard-hat

area," the man continued. Abby recognized the low grumble and gently pushed Matt aside. She grabbed up two of the jugs and started down the aisle.

"Can it, McTavish," she called out. "You're talking to the brass here. He signs the paycheck of the guy who signs your paycheck."

McTavish didn't look impressed. "Well, you still can find yourselves another corner. Some of us have work to do."

"You can get your mind out of the gutter," she told him coolly. She shoved one of the disinfectant containers toward the roll of flesh hanging over the man's belt, forcing him to either grab it or take an uncomfortable blow to the midsection. McTavish caught the container with a grunt.

"McTavish. You tell your boss I sent a requisition in for this stuff two weeks ago, as well as for someone to use it. As usual, I got no response. Now thanks to this department's incompetence, I have a thriving colony of mildew spores over at the arena, a sick dolphin, and contaminated culture swabs. So do you want to get out of my way? Or would you prefer that I fill Mr. Gardner in on the other problems we've had with this department?"

"That him?" McTavish said peering around her. "The guy who's been nosing around, stirring everybody up for the last week?"

Abby nodded. "The man himself."

"Get in line, honey," McTavish said, handing the jug back to her. "I could tell him a thing or two myself. Now get this junk out of here before you spill it on me. Damn stuff gives me hives."

She glanced past him at Matt, who was watching them both with an amused expression. "Mr. Holland's secretary is handling my schedule, Ms. Monroe," he said, his voice revealing no trace of what had passed between them. "Call her for an appointment for an interview on your complaints."

"I already told you—" Abby began.

"For the record," he continued. "And make it today or tomorrow, please. I need to complete my report as soon as possible."

"Of course, Mr. Gardner," she said, though not as coolly as she would have liked. Today or tomorrow? So she could assume he intended to tidy up his business here and move on, just as she'd expected. The thought irritated her, mainly because she'd allowed him to get past her guard.

"And Ms. Monroe?"

"Yes, Mr. Gardner?" she answered, shifting the bottle as she lifted her chin to meet his stare.

"Don't forget to tell your associate to do the same."

"Of course," she answered and turned away. She wasn't sure whether she was being dismissed or protected from gossip, but neither case was acceptable. She picked up the other bottles, balancing two handles in each hand as she slowly faced Matt.

"Mr. Gardner, before I forget, thanks for the flowers," she said. His eyes widened slightly, and she thought she detected a slight twitch at the corner of his mouth.

"I hope you like lilies," he said. "Because I found a nice bunch of them over in the Farm Belt section."

"The daylilies?" she said, pursing her brow in thought as she considered the parallels between the flowers and their relationship. "They're nice while they last, but they only bloom a single day. Then they shrivel up and die."

FIVE

The next morning, a crystal vase with wax daylilies rested atop the small freezer when Abby arrived at the pit. The perfectly shaped blossoms arched naturally, their golden throats glowing with reflected light.

Abby tentatively stroked a soft, delicate petal as a warm wave of pleasure radiated through her. She'd never seen anything quite like these before. They were exquisite.

A door opened and closed on the landing behind her. She turned, drawing a deep, shaky breath when she saw Matt at the top of the stairs. Dressed in twill pants and a black pullover, he looked comfortable, though still overdressed compared with the average park fun seeker. She supposed Matt never would be the kind of man who blended in easily.

"Thank you again for the flowers," she said. "You've gone to a lot of trouble. Why?"

"They're made of beeswax," Matt said, starting down the steps. "They won't shrivel or die. They won't wilt unless you let them melt in the sun." He spoke casually, though the look in his eyes made her want to melt, not into a puddle of wax, but into the heat she'd discovered in his arms. As seductive as the thought was, this was neither the place nor the time. Especially not the time. Why couldn't she have found this man five years ago when she was footloose and happy, not burning with this overwhelming desire to bring another life into the world? She'd have been in a better position to simply enjoy the attention without wondering where it might lead.

"The flowers are beautiful," Abby said. "Where did you find them?"

He shrugged. "In a little shop near my hotel. The owner's a wrinkled old grandmother who looks like she ate too many of her own cookies. She reminds me of my mother, except my mother isn't so talented."

Abby looked up sharply. He so rarely said anything about his family.

"She had a few different kinds but none of these," he continued. "I persuaded her to make these up especially for you."

"That must have cost you a bit," she said softly, touched by the gesture. "Kind of an extravagant way to get your point across."

"Not if the lady gets the message." He plucked one of the golden flowers from the vase and carefully bent a petal around his finger. The soft wax curled, molding to the shape of his flesh.

"I'm not sure what the message is. Could you be more specific? Do you mean one day isn't enough? Or just that fake flowers are more accommodating than real ones, not to mention more expensive?" She turned away with an embarrassed laugh. "I don't even want to consider how that translates to your relationships with women."

He came up behind her, circling her within his arms. The wax lily arched from his fingertips toward her, filling her vision. Its golden throat seemed to glow, drawing energy from his hand. It seemed almost alive.

"This flower is real. It didn't grow this way, but someone with imagination and clever hands made it into the flower you see. It's easy to change. You can leave it like this. Or you can roll it into a warm ball of wax and shape it into whatever you want." He tucked the blossom into her hand and gently turned her in his arms.

"What do you want, Abby Monroe?"

She had to smile. His impatience with fate matched her own. He'd never be one to sit back and let life happen to him. Maybe they had more in common than she'd thought.

"I think I'd scare you away if I told you what I want."

"I don't scare easily."

She leaned back against the sink, away from the seductive heat of his body. But she couldn't escape the heat of his gaze. "I want the quiet magical bond my parents had. I don't know how to explain it. I just know I haven't found it yet, and I won't settle for less."

He reached out, folding her hands between his larger ones. "Maybe if you stop looking so hard, and stop judging, you'll find it right under your nose. That's the thing about magic. It never takes the same shape twice."

Her fingers burned within his grasp, and she pulled them away, suddenly afraid of the emotion surging through her. It felt too close to desire, the blind, unreasoning kind that blocked out logic. She'd learned long ago about desire like that. It led down the path to nowhere.

"I guess that's why people make so many mistakes," she said.

A shadow drifted across his face, then disappeared as quickly as it came. "Maybe, but I just love a challenge," he said.

More flowers appeared the next day, and again the day after that, exquisite creations of colored beeswax in more variations than she'd imagined.

"Somebody has to sign this woman up for the artisan's festival in August. She's good. I wonder if I could get something from her for Starla," Jay said as he rearranged several boxes of fish in the freezer to keep them from falling.

"Maybe a bouquet of stars," Abby suggested. "She might think it's romantic."

Jay picked up the latest bouquet, a tall, slender creation of peach gladiolus blossoms. He twirled it around slowly, then peered at the base of the vase. "Sounds corny. I wonder if she can do roses? Hmm, no name. Matt didn't say where he got these, did he?"

Abby shrugged. "Someplace near his hotel, that's all I know. You could ask him if you can ever catch up with him. You might have better luck checking the Yellow Pages, though."

"Pretty busy, isn't he? I heard a rumor that he's going to have Brett replaced. Any truth to it?"

"I wouldn't know. I haven't had a chance to say more than three words to him lately." She took the vase from Jay and set it carefully on top of the taller of the freezers, well out of harm's way.

The flowers proved he hadn't forgotten her, even though his job seemed to occupy every waking hour. Matt seemed to be everywhere, with his finger on the very pulse of AmericaLand. Already she could sense the change in attitudes of the other workers. Maintenance crews were at work at dawn when she came in early to check on Pepper's cold. They were doing painting touch-ups on overtime hours, authorized by Gardner himself, the crew chief said. Rumor had it that, one by one, the rides would be temporarily closed for complete overhauls and repainting and the adjacent pathways would be repaved. The resulting upswing in morale was manifest in the loud cries of the sideshow barkers and food cart operators throughout the park, not to mention the improved performance of ushers at the dolphin pool.

Of course, Abby appreciated the changes. She didn't know whether Matt was just busy or if he was giving her time to consider what he'd said. But the time away from Matt didn't help her resolve her mixed feelings about the man himself.

Life was what you made it. Fine sentiments, if you could actually live them. She wasn't sure he'd feel the same if she told him what an active hand she'd taken in making her life what she wanted. She didn't have to tell him, or anyone else, about her visits to the clinic yet. Keep it light, he'd said. See what happens. Good advice, she decided.

Jay headed for the administration building immediately after his show with the intention of tracking down the beeswax artist. "Can you cover for me? Starla's birthday is tomorrow. I need to find something for her."

"No problem," Abby said. When he was gone, she pulled out the faded blue swimsuit and quickly changed for a short training session between shows. She saw no sense in letting two hours go to waste, she decided, not when Otto still hadn't mastered his portion of the hoop stunt.

But her thoughts kept drifting back to Matt and this

strange flirtation of theirs. She knew better than to let her attention stray while she was working with the dolphins. But knowing something and actually accomplishing it were two different things, and the training session was wasted. All Abby gained was wrinkled fingers and toes from soaking in the water. Her charges played truant and frolicked around her while her thoughts wandered among the diverse distractions in her life—Matt and the fertility program.

She fluttered her hand through the water to touch her stomach, wondering if a tiny seed might already be growing there. Then she realized she'd unconsciously signaled for the dolphins to perform a series of leaps around the pool. Groaning, she quickly paddled to the middle, treading water and riding the waves as the porpoises circled the pool, frolicking in rehearsed patterns.

"Good, good," she muttered when they finished. She patted each of their beaks when they swam over, nosing her for their reward. She swam to the bucket at the edge and flung a small herring to each of them. Then she ran them through the next set of movements she and Jay had been working on.

It was late evening before she left the dolphin complex, and then it was only to track down supplies to restock the cabinet in the pit. She'd just swiped a pair of scissors from the supply closet across from Bethany's office when Matt found her.

"Now I know why the inventory is in such a mess," he said, coming up behind her quietly. He closed the door, shutting them both in the small, dark space.

"What are you doing?"

"Having a private conversation, I hope."

Abby smiled in the darkness. "No such thing around this place." She felt along the wall until she bumped the light switch. She flicked it on, but nothing happened. "Damn, the light bulb's burned out."

"If you're uncomfortable, we can go into one of the offices," he said.

"It's all right," she said. She wasn't afraid of him. He just made her feel vulnerable, and that meant he could hurt her without even trying.

"There will be gossip about this, you know," she said.

"Nothing worse than the false teeth story, I hope." He sounded amused.

"You probably made that one up yourself."

"Not that one," he said. "Listen, I need to talk to you about a couple of things."

"Business or pleasure?" she said. "By the way, today's flowers were especially lovely. You don't need to keep sending them, though. You have my attention already."

He allowed the silence to settle around them before he spoke. "That's not all I want," he said. His low tenor purred along her nerve endings until she could almost feel the air stirred by his breath brushing against her sensitive skin. He moved closer. Close enough to touch, but not touching, as before. She didn't feel crowded, though she knew she should.

"Better handle business first," she suggested, pulling herself back to reality.

"Maybe you're right," he said, regret lacing through his words. "I need to ask you about something I found in your file."

A chill chased away Abby's smile. She didn't want anyone looking into her file, not at the insurance records or the copies of medical claims filed earlier this year through the company's insurance policy. Those were no one's business but her own. The records of the cyst removal could lead to supposition about her current relationship with the clinic. Also, there were letters calling her current employment into question, letters that could get her transferred from this park and away from the fertility program.

"What's so interesting about my file?" she demanded, trying to sound casual.

"Mostly your address and telephone number," he teased. His lighter tone fell on dead silence. "Not funny. Okay, I'm interested in the citation for insubordination."

Her unease increased. "Oh, that. I didn't pay too much attention when I got my copy. I cleared my actions with my supervisor at Marine Shows."

"Brett said you ignored his orders on three separate occasions, that you went over your budget and charged unnecessary supplies to AmericaLand accounts, and that you physically assaulted him."

She felt the old anger rising again and fought it down. "So, what's your point?" she said. She'd been right. Beneath the laughter and the heat of his kiss lurked a corporate shark. And smart women didn't play with sharks.

"Is it true?"

"Yes," she answered, feeling another of her dreams shrivel and die within her. Against her better judgment, she'd let this man behind her guard. And she'd begun to hope he might be the one she'd been waiting for.

"All of it?" he asked.

She grabbed the doorknob, twisting it open. "You read the file. You obviously talked to Brett." She started to leave, but he tugged her back in, slamming the door. The light blinked on.

"It figures," she muttered. "Just another thing that

never got fixed.'' Abby blinked angrily at Matt's amused expression.

''I assume you had a good reason for assaulting him.''

''Damned right I did,'' she retorted, planting her fists on her hips. ''But the supposed assault was four years ago. The citation was last year. He threatened it, and I ignored him. It was that or buy the pool chemicals myself, but my credit card was already at the limit. Of course, I could have let the dolphin water turn green with algae and risked having Otto and Pepper get bacterial infections.''

Matt's grin had widened while she talked until he practically beamed. ''Why didn't you file a formal complaint with headquarters?''

''I did. I never heard back from them.''

''Did you mail it out of this office?''

She thought back, trying to remember. ''Probably. I typed it in Bethany's office.''

''And you mailed it from here?''

She shook her head. ''Certified mail via the post office in my neighborhood. I still have the return receipt. When nobody responded, I figured Brett acted according to company policy.''

Matt shook his head. ''It appears the problem is a little bigger than we first thought.''

''Meaning?''

He shook his head. ''You know better than to ask that. All I can say is this job is going to take a lot longer than I first expected. I might be around for quite a while yet.''

''Am I supposed to construe that as good news?''

''Not for the company,'' he replied. ''Personally, I consider it great news. I get a chance to see you every day for several weeks, maybe even longer if I talk loud and fast enough. It gives me time to collect on that dinner."

She stared hard for a moment, then let her lips relax into a smile. "I think it's time I paid up on our deal. How about Saturday night at my house? I can't promise gourmet cooking or four-star service, but at least it'll be away from the park."

"I guess this means you're willing to take a chance and see what happens."

"I'll play along for a while," she agreed.

"Good." Matt gently tapped her chin, then trailed his fingers along her jawline to her ear and back again. He dropped a light kiss onto her forehead, then her lips, lingering just long enough to cloud her thoughts with a taste of desire.

"I hope you hit him really hard," he said. He opened the door, leaving her standing alone in the closet, with the forgotten scissors balanced in her hand.

Pop was giving the shrubs their weekly trim when Abby returned home after her Friday afternoon appointment at the clinic. He waved absently, barely looking away from his snipping shears. She eased her newly repaired car down the narrow driveway beside the 1940s bungalow and halted next to the back sidewalk.

She shot her father an irritated look as she unstuck her thighs from the seat and climbed out. She didn't care what Pop said. The vinyl seats were a mistake.

Maybe this was a sign. Maybe she should have blown Aunt Margaret's money on a sporty model with comfortable leather seats. At least she'd have a sure thing instead of the maybe-this-time-maybe-not routine the doctor had given her. But a sports car wouldn't have chubby perfect toes or give hugs that could bring tears to her eyes. And it wouldn't grow into an inquisitive little imp like her nephews. She wondered if Pop would ever truly understand how badly she wanted a child. He claimed his own three children were unplanned gifts from God. For Abby, the only real difference was in the planning.

She grabbed both bags of groceries from the back seat and started for the front door. By the time she reached the bottom step, one bag had slipped out of her grasp. She stopped to hitch it up, fumbling awkwardly with it.

"Here, I'll get that," her father said, taking it from her. "It's about time you got home. You run into trouble at the clinic?"

"No, I spent too much time at the store, trying to decide what to have for dinner tomorrow night."

He pulled a smaller pharmacy bag out of the larger brown grocery sack. "What's this?"

She hesitated, then relented. "A pregnancy test."

He snorted. "Can't you wait to find out the usual way?"

"No, I can't," she retorted. "This test is supposed to show accurate results within ten days after conception."

"Why did you buy it now?"

Abby glared in exasperation as she stalked past. "Because it was on sale. What do you think?"

"I think you just couldn't wait," he said with a bland look. "By the way, the kids have called twice. You baby-sitting tonight?"

Abby nodded. "Maureen and John have some sort of company dinner. So I told the kids I'd take them to play miniature golf."

Pop nodded. "Well, if you bring them here afterwards, don't let them make a mess. I just got the place cleaned up."

Abby rolled her eyes. "They're your grandchildren."

"And I love them. Keep them outside in the yard if you bring them over," he said. "Out of my roses, too." He paused at the doorway, fishing in the bag, his bushy eyebrows pinching together in a frown.

"I didn't forget your cigars. They're in there somewhere," she said.

"What's this?" He pulled out the bottle of Chianti and frowned. "You stay out of this stuff, just in case you're already pregnant."

"It's for dinner tomorrow, Pop. Don't tell me you forgot Matt's coming over."

"I didn't forget. That's why I was trimming the shrubs. I dusted, too. Didn't want him to think the Monroes lived like slobs," he said.

"I thought you cleaned up because Reverend Carpenter is stopping by."

"That, too," he said, then gave a grunt of satisfaction as he found the cigars. He pulled a single panatela from the box and smiled. "Might as well enjoy 'em now. Can't be smoking these around a new baby."

Abby hesitated. "Does this mean you're starting to like the idea?"

"Of my daughter raising a child alone? Not a bit. But you're as bullheaded as your mother." His wrinkled frown deepened, tightening the lines around his mouth. He bit down on the end of the panatela and grunted. "Come to think of it, you're more like the woman every day. I'll probably have to give these up before the baby's even born. Made your mother sick as a drunk on the morning after."

"Dad!" He held the door wide, letting her pass through in front of them.

"Just the smell of them made her turn green," he said. "You sure you want to do this? Your mother had terrible morning sickness."

Abby set the groceries on the kitchen counter and turned to face him, hands on her hips. ''It's a little late to change my mind. Either I'm pregnant or I'm not. It's just a matter of waiting now.''

''And if you're not? You're prepared for that, aren't you?'' He looked unsure of himself, caught between concern and lingering outrage. ''I read a little out of those books you brought home. This isn't a sure thing.''

''We already discussed this,'' she said. ''I'll just try again, as many times as it takes or until Aunt Margaret's money runs out.''

He jammed the cigar back into his mouth. ''You always were the impatient one.''

''So you say,'' she muttered, turning her back on him as she carried the groceries into the tiny walk-in pantry just off the kitchen. She heard him shuffle over to the refrigerator, grumbling under his breath.

''Hey, Pop,'' she called as she leaned around the corner. ''Are you going to accept Reverend Carpenter's offer about the youth group?''

He gave her a skeptical look. ''Well, I don't know. There's this baby business. I'm not sure what kind of an example our family would be setting for these kids.''

''Have you told him?''

''I suppose I should. I just haven't figured out how yet. Thought I'd just wait to see what happens.''

Abby knew what he meant. Pop saw no sense in telling anyone until the procedure proved successful. If it wasn't, nobody would be the wiser and he'd forego the embarrassment.

''Oh, Daddy.'' She knew her decision would affect her family, but this was one aspect she hadn't anticipated.

He caught her by the shoulders. ''Never mind. What's

done is done. I don't understand it, but I'll stand by you."

She hugged him tightly. "That's all I ask," she said. She pulled away before he could see the tears welling up in her eyes. Stepping quickly into the pantry, she wiped at her eyes, then started to put the groceries away. She'd barely finished with the first bag when the doorbell chimed.

"Get that, will you? I need to change my shirt before I talk to Reverend Carpenter."

Abby left the remaining bag of groceries in the pantry. "What are you going to tell him?"

"I said I haven't decided. Now hurry and let the man in." He watched her with a worried expression. "Don't know what the world's coming to," he muttered.

She hesitated, then pressed a quick kiss to his cheek. He wasn't enthusiastic, but at least he'd stopped yelling and trying to talk her out of it. He'd come around when that tiny baby hand closed around his finger. Maybe sooner, she decided as she hurried down the hallway to the front door.

"Give him some iced tea and tell him I'll be out in a minute," her father called after her.

"Right." She swung the door open and smiled at her father's friend and confidant. Reverend Carpenter wasn't alone, though. Behind the kindly gray-haired minister stood Matt Gardner, with the devil's mischief twinkling in his eyes. He certainly had the devil's sense of timing, she thought, always turning up when she least expected him.

"Ah, there is someone at home," Reverend Carpenter said, removing his Royals' baseball cap as he stepped onto the polished parquet entry. "I was just telling Mr. Gardner here that we should check the backyard to see if your father was perhaps out in the garden. Jake is quite a gardener. Oh, goodness. That's quite a coincidence. Gardner, gardener."

Abby laughed weakly, looking from one to the other. "Yes, isn't it?"

"You look surprised."

"I am. I just got home and—"

"You weren't expecting me," Matt filled in. "Your father didn't tell you I called?"

"I guess he forgot," she said. "Never mind. Make yourself at home. I take it you've already met Reverend Carpenter."

"I drove in behind him. We've only had time to exchange names, professions, and baseball favorites. I'm a Mets' man myself."

"Only because he doesn't know any better yet," Reverend Carpenter interjected. "Come to the game on Saturday. We'll show you how baseball is really played."

Matt's warm glance fell on Abby. "Maybe next time. I have plans for Saturday already."

Seeing the older man's speculative glance, she decided she'd better explain before he jumped to any unwelcome conclusions. "Matt's from New York. He's working out at the park for a few weeks."

"Ah, that explains his misguided loyalties."

Matt chuckled, running a hand through his hair. "One man's opinion," he answered. He pushed the door closed behind them, shutting out the glare of the July sun. In the softer light filtering through the curtains, the devilish look faded to warm interest. Damn, but she wished he wouldn't look at her that way, not with the man who had christened her standing not three feet away.

"Besides," the older man continued as he shuffled heavily toward his customary seat by the window, "I don't believe I've heard much about you. Have you been seeing Abby for a while now?"

She threw an apologetic look in Matt's direction. "Sorry," she said. "He's almost a part of the family."

"Don't worry. I just stopped by to see if you'd like to go paddling this afternoon. I heard they rent canoes at Longview Lake."

She shook her head. "I can't. I promised my nephews I'd take them to play miniature golf."

He hesitated, studying her. "Would I be intruding if I invited myself along?"

"Not if you spring for ice cream afterward." She crossed her arms, waiting to see whether he'd pass this test. If he didn't, he could take his charming brown eyes and his kisses elsewhere. She had little room in her life for a man who didn't like children.

"How many nephews?"

"Two. Steven is eight years old, and his little brother Eric is seven." If that didn't discourage him, nothing would. She watched him carefully, searching for hesitancy.

Amusement flashed through Matt's eyes and in the upturned corners of his mouth. "Nothing I can't handle."

"That's what I'm afraid of. You'll probably teach them new tricks," she said. "Have a seat and I'll get you something to drink. Pop should be out any minute."

"I'll help you," Matt offered.

"No, please," she said, pushing him firmly into a chair. "Keep the Reverend company. I'll just be a moment." She leaned closer, whispering low in his ear. "It's the price of arriving unexpectedly."

Matt gave a low, intimate chuckle as she drew away. "So tell me, Reverend Carpenter, what was Abby like as a child?"

She groaned and fled the room. She met her father in the hallway, still buttoning the crisp white shirt he'd changed into. "Pop, didn't you have a message for me?"

Irritation flashed across her father's expressive face. "From that Matt fellow? Yeah, he said he might be by here this afternoon. I told him to come whenever he finished with his work."

"Thanks for the warning," she replied sarcastically. "He's here now."

His expression cleared. "Is he? My, this could be serious. It's only been an hour or so since he called. Is he the one who walked you out that time I took you to the clinic?"

"Yes, but don't get your hopes up. And don't mention the baby," Abby ground out, feeling herself flush.

"We don't know there's a baby yet," he reminded her. "By the way, have you told Matt what you're planning?"

"We're not that close," she said.

"But he makes your face flush and your heart patter along, now doesn't he?"

"Never mind, Pop. It's my business, not yours."

Her father reared back, looking down his long nose at her. "Where is this man of yours?"

She heaved an exasperated sigh. "He's in the living room with Reverend Carpenter now. Please, don't get the baby pictures out and don't let the Reverend tell him about the time Bethany and I got caught skinny-dipping at church camp."

"Just get the tea," he said with a small knowing smile.

She hurried into the kitchen, ignoring the low chuckle floating down the hallway after her. She nearly broke a glass in her rush to get the drinks and return to the living room. She didn't want to leave Matt at the mercy of the two older men and their not-so-subtle questions about his intentions. As she worked, she could hear them talking but couldn't make out more than an occasional word.

Two minutes later, she stepped through the arched doorway into the living room, bearing a tray of filled glasses. To her relief, Matt seemed perfectly at ease, sitting in the overstuffed chair by the window while the two older men argued on the couch. She noticed her father had finally lit the cigar.

"What do you mean you don't have any experience? Jake, you've raised three daughters. You have grandchildren," Reverend Carpenter was saying.

Her father took a long puff on the cigar, then leaned back, blowing smoke rings into the air with the showmanship of a circus ringmaster. "You see that? I blow a little smoke and the grandchildren think I'm the greatest thing since grilled-cheese sandwiches. When they get out of line, I swat them on the behind. It's not the same with these older kids. I don't understand 'em, not their music, not the way they talk." He took a glass from the tray, then waited for the others to do the same. "I'm not the person you need," he added.

"I disagree," Abby said as she settled into her mother's cushioned rocker. "You'd be great. And they're good kids."

"We all want to keep them that way," the Reverend said.

Pop nodded. "I understand that. There are other reasons, though."

Abby leaned forward, suddenly uneasy. Surely he wouldn't tell them about the fertility program now. "Pop," she said in a low voice.

"I may be out of town for a while," he said. "I don't want to get started on something when I may not be able to follow through."

"Planning a trip?" Matt asked.

She smiled in relief. "Are you finally going to take that cruise?"

"Nope. I thought maybe I'd come with you when you move the dolphins to the Tulsa aquarium for the winter. I'm getting too old for shoveling snow and all that nonsense."

"Oh." She sat back, trying to absorb the implications of this idea. "Are you serious?"

He blew another puff of smoke into the air, then stubbed out the cigar in his wife's crystal ashtray. "We'll see how it goes," he said.

"It snows in Tulsa," Abby reminded him.

"The wind isn't so bitter," Pop said. "So you see, Reverend, I'd be happy to help out whenever I can. I just wouldn't want anyone to depend on me for a permanent commitment."

"Well, I'll put you down as one of the chaperones," the man said.

Her father cast a resigned look about the room and grunted. "For now," he agreed. "To change the subject, I want you to take a look at my roses. There's some kind of bug eating the buds."

Reverend Carpenter's gaze sharpened. "You don't say. Not aphids, I hope. They've been terrible this year."

"Something else. Matt, Abby, are you coming or do you want to stay in here?" Pop's expression remained bland, though Abby caught the calculating glimmer in his eyes as he surveyed Matt, from his designer-label polo shirt to the tips of his Gucci loafers. "Or would you two rather stay in here and talk in private?"

She tilted her head suspiciously. "Matchmaking again, Pop? Watch out, Matt. He's already measuring you for a tux."

Matt laughed easily as he stood and held out a hand to her father. "Nice to meet you, Mr. Monroe. I'll see you again tomorrow if not sooner."

"You and Abby got a date? They do still call them dates, don't they?" Reverend Carpenter asked. "Sometimes I lose track of the lingo."

"Abby's paying up on a bargain we made. She's cooking me dinner. Italian, I hope."

Jake turned away, shaking his head. "Oh, boy. We're in trouble now."

SIX

After two hours of miniature golf in the late afternoon sunshine, the cool interior of the snack bar at Merlin's Emporium felt wonderful. While Matt got the boys ice cream, Abby picked out a booth in the corner, as far away from the noise of the arcade room as possible. She had to wait only a few minutes before the others joined her. She used the time to recover from the heat and wonder about Matt's attitude.

He'd shown more energy and enthusiasm for the golf game than even the boys. In fact, he'd been brimming with a caged energy ever since he'd shown up at the house earlier this afternoon. Even now, as he pointed the boys toward the table, he moved with a lift to his step.

''Eric said you like chocolate,'' Matt said, handing her a double-scoop cone.

''Good job, Eric,'' she said, winking at the seven-year-old sliding into the seat next to her. She eyed the single dip on his cone, then noticed that everyone else had single dips, too. Matt burst into laughter when her accusing gaze fell on him. "Are you trying to tell me something?"

"Don't blame me," he said. "They insisted you always get two dips."

"You always pig out on chocolate," eight-year-old Steven said. He stuffed the top of the cone in his mouth, making loud, slurping noises.

"Talk about pigs," Abby muttered. "You're lucky your mother isn't here."

"You're more fun," Eric assured her, right before he bit down on his own cone, half swallowing the top.

"Yeah, Mom makes us get frozen yogurt. Ice cream's better," Steven piped in.

"More fun. See, it's easy to be a favorite aunt. I know all the tricks," she said, her gaze swiveling back to Matt. His amusement under control, he was taking slow, measured swipes at his own cone. She wondered whether he only ate ice cream and kissed with such masterful deliberation or whether that approach extended to every part of his life.

Another loud slurp from Eric reminded her that she had no business thinking in those terms right now. She forced her attention back to the small boy beside her.

"Eric, your mom said you went on the Scout campout last weekend."

"Yeah, they let the little kids go when it's warm outside," Steven piped in. "He fell in the creek and almost drowned."

"Did not!"

"You did, too. Dad had to pull you out."

"That's 'cause Dicky Barnum was sitting on my stomach."

Abby frowned down at Eric. "Is he the boy who glued your hamster to the wall?"

Matt's eyes widened. "You're making this up,

right?" His knee bumped against hers, the denim rubbing coarsely against her smooth skin.

"Nope." She shifted to give his longer legs more room under the narrow table, but he bumped against her again.

"I glued Dicky's pants to his chair the next day to get back at him," Eric said, with so much enthusiasm that Abby thought he might bury the remains of his cone in her hair. She rescued the sticky mess, directing the cone toward his mouth.

"Aren't kids great? Makes you want a couple of your own," she said. Oddly enough, spending time with these two little monsters didn't dampen her enthusiasm for motherhood in the least. Even at their most exasperating, they were more interesting than most of the adults she knew. They certainly were more entertaining.

Matt chuckled wryly. "Do you want to live like this every day?" He had finished his own cone and was wiping up the chocolate drips on the table in front of the boys.

"Only on weekends. Too much fun will turn them into spoiled monsters," she countered.

"I want to do this every day," Steven said.

Matt's dark brow lifted. "I'll just bet you would. What about school? What about a job?"

"I don't have a job. I'm a kid," Steven retorted.

"Well, eat your ice cream, kid," he said. He ceremoniously popped the last of his own cone into his mouth. He held it there for a moment, his eyelids drooping closed in nostalgic bliss, as if repeating a simple childhood ritual. The lines across his brow had almost vanished, giving the impression he was enjoying himself far more than either of them expected. She realized there was something irresistible about a man who enjoyed children.

His eyes opened again, catching her staring. Afraid her expression might reveal too much, she looked quickly down at her cone and licked around the melting edge. Her gaze kept straying back to Matt though. Each time, his smile was a little bit wider, until she stopped, lowering the cone and reaching for a napkin.

"I have it on my face, don't I?" She dabbed at her chin.

"No. I just like looking at you," he said. "You have a very expressive face. But I suppose you know that, having been an actress."

"It was just dinner theater," she reminded him. "And I wasn't very good."

He looked unconvinced. "You must have been. You put on a great show with the dolphins, and not always under the best of circumstances. You make your audience think everything is going according to plan, even when Otto refuses to obey you. That takes real talent."

"Otto's young. Covering for him is part of the job." Embarrassed, she pretended to concentrate on what Eric was saying. But the little-boy chatter skipped in one ear and out the other like background music for her thoughts.

Matt shifted, bumping against her leg again. His broad grin told her he'd done it on purpose. She shot him a warning look, but he ignored her and rubbed his leg against hers. She kicked him under the table, not hard enough to do any serious damage, but hard enough for him to get the message.

"There are children around," she said quietly.

He nodded. "Right, for now," he said, propping both elbows on the table as he leaned toward her nephews. "Boys, tell me about this creek where you went camping." A moment later, he was trading camping stories with both boys and impressing the heck out of them if their expressions were any indication.

Abby licked another drip of chocolate, then gave up the battle against the heat and the soggy cone in her hand. She reached over the back of the booth and dumped it into a dirty cup on the empty table behind her. While she wiped the stickiness from her fingers, she listened as Matt told an old ghost story, one of the gory summer camp tales about the escaped convict who supposedly lurked in the woods. She had to admit, he knew exactly how to distract them into behaving themselves. He held their attention, talking on their level but not down to them. He treated them like people, which was what they were beneath that tough little-boy bluster.

A blast of air-conditioning blew directly on the table from an overhead vent, disturbing the loose waves of Matt's windblown hair. A tuft fluttered on his forehead, drawing her gaze. It wasn't just brown, she decided, but a rich coffee color with sunburnt tips. The same color as the baby sea otter she'd helped nurse to health when she'd volunteered at the Tulsa zoo last winter. She wondered if Matt's hair would be as soft as that baby's thick fur.

Her focus shifted slightly lower, centering on his eyes. Slightly darker than his hair, they sparkled with laughter as he responded to something one of the boys said. Then suddenly, those eyes locked with hers.

"Well, Aunt Abby, did you?" Eric demanded.

"Yes, Aunt Abby, is it true?" Matt asked, his voice sliding into that low purr she'd come to equate with his slow seduction of her senses. It was almost enough to make her forget the boys were there.

"Is what true?"

"That Reverend Carpenter caught you and Aunt

Bethany swimming naked at church camp," Steven said.

She blinked with surprise. Leave it to the children to tell the family secrets. "Where did you hear about that, young man?" Probably listening at the keyhole when they should have been asleep, she guessed.

"Grandpa told Daddy about it. He said Mommy got poison ivy all over one time, too," Steven said.

"What's poison ivy?" Eric demanded.

Abby laughed. "An itchy rash, something you don't want to get. What else have you heard lately that you shouldn't have?"

"Nothing." They both replied with suddenly angelic expressions. Matt took one look at them and started laughing.

"Right. And I'm a purple people eater," she muttered wryly.

Eric tapped her arm. "Mommy and Daddy were whispering about you last night."

"I don't think I want to hear this," Abby muttered. Steven leaned forward, his face a picture of eager anticipation. Eric, though, just looked puzzled.

"They were in the kitchen," Eric continued. "Mommy said you were buying a baby. Where do you buy babies?"

Abby gasped, then choked. She grabbed a handful of napkins and covered her mouth, coughing hard. Matt started to rise, but she waved him back into his seat and swallowed hard, trying to regain control of herself. By the time she could breathe, both boys were staring at her, looking pale and worried.

"I'm fine," she assured them, her voice still scratchy.

"You're sure?" Matt asked.

"Yeah, your face looks really red and splotchy," Steven said.

She grimaced at her nephew, then drew a deep

breath. She puffed out her cheeks, crossed her eyes, and slumped onto the seat. Both boys erupted into fits of laughter. After a brief look of disbelief, Matt just grinned.

"Now I know your secret," he said.

"Yeah, drop to their level and distract them," she said. "A little trick I picked up working in children's theater one summer."

She sat up straight and reached for her purse. Pulling out a roll of quarters, she doled out eight to each of the boys. "There you go. Don't come back until you run out of money or it's six o'clock, whichever comes first," she said.

"Six o'clock?" Matt said, eyeing her with skepticism as the boys raced around the tables into the arcade room at the other side of the snack bar.

She shook her head. "Don't worry. Neither of them is very good. They'll be done in a half hour, forty-five minutes at the most."

Matt braced his elbows on the table and leaned closer. "Whatever," he said, his eyes sparkling with amusement. "So tell me. Where *do* you buy babies?"

Abby stared at him for a long moment. He thought it was a joke, something overheard and misunderstood. It was a reasonable assumption, considering the question had come from a seven-year-old. She'd treat it as a joke for now.

She sent him a smoky look and batted her eyelashes. "Are you in the market for one?" she asked in the breathiest, sultriest voice she could manage.

His eyes crinkled with laughter. "It depends on what I have to do to get one," he replied.

She hesitated, then shook her head. "Nope, I don't want to take this conversation any further," she said. "I just wonder exactly what Eric overhead." She also wondered what Matt would think if he knew how close Eric had come to the truth. Now wasn't the time to find out, she decided. Not here, with all these people.

She pulled out a few more quarters and headed for the old-fashioned jukebox situated along the far wall. She leaned over, searching the selections for something quiet.

"What do you want to hear?" she asked as Matt came up behind her. He drew closer, bumping against her and nestling his chin on her shoulder as he checked out the offerings.

"You choose," he said.

She glanced around the room. It was almost empty, except for a group of teenage girls in spandex in one corner and a pair of grandparents in baggy cotton across from them. A diverse group with diverse tastes, she decided.

"Something quiet," she said. She punched a series of buttons, then sidestepped away from Matt's touch. He stared down at the jukebox a moment longer, then added his own quarter.

Then he straightened and slowly ambled back to the booth and slid into the seat opposite her. This time, when he nuzzled her leg beneath the table, she bumped him back and let a slow, mischievous smile curve her lips.

"We're still in a public place," she reminded him.

"And if we weren't?"

She hesitated. "I might be tempted. What song did you pick just now?"

" 'Angel Kisses.' I thought it sounded appropriate for a certain lady who keeps changing the subject. Why?"

"Maybe the subject needs changing," she replied.

"Do I make you uncomfortable?"

"No. It's just that one of us has to keep a grip on reality. An affair with a businessman who's passing through isn't part of my master plan."

"What if I told you I might be around longer than I first expected?"

Abby considered a moment. "Will you?"

He nodded. "I'm replacing Brett until the end of the season. After that, who knows?"

That could explain his exuberant mood this afternoon. He seemed extraordinarily pleased with the course of events, so pleased that she wondered how he'd held the news in for the last couple of hours.

Unless he'd known for some time. Unless that was the overall plan. The thought put a whole new light on their relationship, on his pursuit of her.

"How long have you known this?"

"You sound suspicious. What are you thinking?"

"That your interest in me coincides neatly with this extended assignment in Kansas City," she said carefully. "I wonder if you'd have gone to so much trouble if you were returning to New York on Monday. Or maybe you just enjoy the chase, the game as you call it." That was putting it bluntly, but she suspected he preferred honesty over platitudes.

"You should know better by now," he replied.

"I've met my share of smooth talkers," she answered. "I've learned to be careful."

He leaned forward and grasped her hand. He placed it, palm down, against his chest. She could feel the warm heat of him through the thin shirt, the firm flesh beneath it. And she could feel the frantic beat of his heart.

"There," he said. "That's why I'm here. I can't decide whether I feel like a kid with his first crush or a man who's become obsessed with something he can't have. I just know that when you touch me, my pulse goes crazy. When we kiss, it's like nothing I've ever felt before."

She looked away, unable to face the fire burning in his eyes and still keep her common sense in control. "It's physical, chemical, just hormones."

He lifted her hand and she felt his kiss on her fingertips, melting the last of her resistance. She took his hands, grasping earnestly as she struggled to maintain her sense of perspective.

"You're the one who said keep it light. Just see how things go. After dinner tomorrow night, you might never want to see me or my family again."

He leaned closer, touching his lips briefly to hers. "Don't count on it. I very much like what I've seen so far. That's one of the reasons why I asked for the manager's job. I want to give us time to find out what's going on between us, to enjoy it. Even if it doesn't last, we could have a hell of a time making memories."

Abby drew a deep, shaky breath. Her heart felt as if it was turning over inside her rib cage. She could very easily fall in love with this man. She was already halfway there.

She lifted her gaze, studying his face for the sincerity she heard in his voice. His expression was a reflection of her own emotions. Heat. Desire. Pure passion. And something that looked close to love. She blinked, partly in surprise and partly in disbelief.

Then Matt looked away and groaned. "And now, our time is up."

Abby sighed and turned to face her nephews, glad they were too young to read the emotions that must be clearly displayed on her face.

"Can we have more quarters?" Steven asked.

"Not a chance," she said. "It's time to go see

Grandpa. I talked him into renting a tape for you, Ninja something or other."

"All right!" both boys yelled in unison as they slapped their hands together in a high salute.

"I like your family," Matt whispered the following evening. He stood close behind her as she stirred the bubbling pot of spaghetti sauce. They were alone in the kitchen for the moment, though Abby expected that to change at any time.

"I think my family likes you, too," she replied, feeling a warm wave of pleasure that was all tangled up with his nearness and the easy way he'd insinuated himself into the Monroe household. Since Matt had arrived two hours ago, they'd had no more than a moment of peace from the rest of her family. Finally, though, they'd all gone home, leaving just Pop in the house with them.

Pop hadn't said much, but she could tell by the casual way he put Matt to work in the garden that he approved of him. Twice, she'd caught Pop watching Matt with a speculative gleam in his eyes. She knew what he was thinking, because she'd thought it, too. No matter what she'd said aloud, she'd secretly wondered if Matt could be the one, the man with the power to either share her dreams or break her heart.

Matt rested a hand on her shoulder, gently massaging. "You look like you belong here, almost domestic," he said. "I don't understand why your father keeps making nasty remarks about your cooking."

She swung around, fitting herself into the circle of his arms. "I have a confession to make. I wasn't slaving away in the kitchen while you helped Pop. I watched a PBS special on whales."

He pulled her closer against him. "You watched television? While I sweated in the sun trying to impress your father, you sat in front of the fan and watched whales leap through the arctic water?''

Abby giggled. ''Not exactly.''

''What did you do? Call the caterer? You are a clever one, aren't you?'' He sounded almost approving. The corporate mind-set again, she surmised. Efficient use of time and resources brought high marks, and that included using the skills of professionals whenever necessary.

''The meatballs came frozen,'' she explained. ''The sauce came in a can. I just chopped a little basil and oregano from the garden and threw them in.''

''You're cooking the pasta, aren't you?''

She glanced over her shoulder, then twisted quickly to turn off the flame beneath the tall stainless steel pot. ''Boiling it over,'' she remarked. ''Don't say you weren't warned. We might have soggy spaghetti yet.''

He picked up the long wooden spoon and swirled it through the frothy water, capturing several long strands and lifting them from the water. ''My father used to fling it against the wall to see if it would stick. If it wouldn't, it wasn't ready.''

She took the spoon away from him and dropped the spaghetti back into the water. ''I hope your mother made him clean the wall.''

''Actually, I'm not sure she ever knew. He only made spaghetti when Mom wasn't there. My sister had trouble eating it, but Dad always said she needed a little adventure in her life, just like everyone else.''

''I guess she was still small then.'' Abby stirred the sauce again, pretending nonchalance. She wanted to know about his family, just as he was learning about hers. But she didn't want to press too hard. She looked up, catching his troubled look.

"Don't. I'm pushing, aren't I? I'm sorry," she said. She touched his cheek, then stroked away the lines fanning away from the corners of his eyes. And the sadness faded some.

"It's all right. My sister was disabled. She didn't live to be very old," he explained. "Besides, Dad isn't much of a cook. Spaghetti's easy to fix, almost foolproof, no offense intended," he said, with a sideways glance at her.

She smiled, letting him draw the subject away from more painful memories. "I could ruin it yet. Why don't you save our dinner and drain the spaghetti? There's a strainer in the sink already," she said, crossing the room to the refrigerator.

"You can't convince me that you're incompetent at anything."

She pulled out a foil-wrapped loaf of garlic bread. She bumped the door closed with a light swing of the hip. "Pop has a theory about us girls. Our mom was perfect, and she split all her good points between us. Bethany got the responsible genes. Maureen got domestic ones."

"Which genes did you get?"

She answered with a mischievous smile. "I'm fun, remember?"

"Fun? I'll show you fun." A cloud of steam billowed around him as he leaned over the sink, tilting the huge pan. He emptied it with a flourish. Then he dropped the pot on the counter with a clatter and stalked purposefully toward her, brandishing the oven mitts with mock menace.

She giggled and slapped at him with the bread. He snatched it from her and dropped it onto the table. "That's just slapstick," she taunted. "Anybody can do slapstick."

He tossed the mitts after the bread, then leaped with unexpected speed, catching her and trapping her against the wall. She leaned back, feeling the rasp of the bumpy plaster through the thin blouse.

"Now what?" she said, lifting her chin in challenge. "Are you going to overwhelm me with your charm or tickle me into submission?"

"Ooo, you're tough," he said, leaning closer to brush his lips against hers. "You're it." He sprang away from her, backing around the table with a bouncing boxer's step, ready to feint and dodge.

"It?"

"Yeah, tag, you're it." His chin tilted at a cocky angle, challenging her.

She grinned, feinted to the left, then ran to the right, circling the table.

"Missed," he called, then danced through the doorway and down the hall with Abby hot on his heels. The chase continued out the front door, around the house, and into the backyard before she caught him in the kitchen doorway. She grabbed onto his shirttail, tugging lightly, and dodged away from his grasping hands as he spun around. She turned to run and bumped hard into her father's solid frame.

"Oops, sorry Pop," she said, steadying herself with a hand to his arm.

He looked from one to the other, shaking his head in resignation. "Worse than the grandkids," he muttered, though he looked pleased, as if he'd organized the impromptu chase.

"Just trying to keep your daughter in line," Matt remarked. He strode over to the sink and upended the spaghetti strainer over the big pot. The pasta stuck, then plopped in a lump into the pot with a dull plunk.

"Whatever you want to call it," Pop said. "Matt,

you have a phone call. You can take it in the den or you can take it in here, whatever you want.''

''In here's fine,'' Matt said, wiping his hands on a towel. As he picked up the receiver, his manner underwent a subtle change, sobering into that of the corporate troubleshooter she'd first met. A moment later he relaxed.

''It's nice to talk to you, too, Steven,'' he said. ''What can I do for you?''

Abby turned to her father with a questioning look.

''Seems your friend here made quite an impression on the kids,'' he said. ''Maureen says they've been talking about him all day. Young Steven there had some burning question that couldn't wait.''

''Matt really surprised me yesterday,'' she admitted. ''He seemed to enjoy spending time with the boys.''

Pop emitted a low grunt. ''Could be you jumped the gun on this baby thing.''

''Shh,'' she ordered, turning to see if Matt had overheard. But he was listening intently, a strange expression on his face.

''No, Dicky Barnum is wrong. Kissing does not make your lips fall off. I promise you, neither Aunt Abby nor I will be deformed. Why would you believe somebody who glues small animals to walls, anyway?''

Abby covered her mouth, trying not to laugh as she turned to her father. Pop simply rolled his eyes, then pointed a stubby finger at her. ''Watch yourself, girl. You used to think earthworms grew up and became garter snakes.''

''I don't think that's so funny,'' she whispered after him as he left the room. ''It's a reasonable assumption for a four-year-old.''

''You were six,'' Pop said, turning to leave.

''I couldn't have been.'' She crossed her arms,

frowning after her father as he walked stiffly down the hall, favoring his right leg. He'd overdone it in the garden this afternoon. She picked up the bread from the table and put it in the already hot oven, then retrieved the spaghetti. A little canola oil and a light stirring separated most of the strands, making the pasta a bit more appealing.

She was dumping the sauce into a serving bowl when Matt hung up the phone. "Everything straightened out?" she asked.

He nodded. "Evidently your nephews were watching when I said good-bye yesterday. Kids get things pretty twisted sometimes."

"Especially when they have friends like Dicky Barnum," she replied. "Do you want to help me set the table?" She handed him a short stack of plates before he could answer, then reached into the silverware drawer. Behind her, she heard the soft clunk of stoneware as he followed her directions. She briskly gathered the silverware into one hand, grabbed the napkins, and started for the table.

"For somebody with no time for a family, you seem to know a lot about children. You certainly handled Steven and Eric well yesterday," she said, brushing past him.

"I've been around kids before. I used to date a woman who had kids."

"Boys?"

"A boy and a girl, about the same ages as your nephews. I spent a lot of time with them, both by myself and doing family-type stuff. Baseball games, ice cream in the park, Disney movies. Actually, it was one of the better times of my life."

Abby watched him carefully, sensing no discomfort

on his part, only a faint hint of regret in his expression. "What happened?"

"She wanted something more permanent, more kids, a house in the suburbs, the great American dream."

"And you didn't," she finished for him. "She had children, you didn't want to be a father. Is that it?" She hoped not. She didn't want to care so much for a man who didn't want to raise children.

He eyed her sharply. "Not exactly. I cared about her a great deal, and I cared about her children. I still do. I send them birthday presents and show up on their doorstep every Christmas morning at six A.M."

"Sounds as if you still have some pretty strong feelings for this woman," she said. The thought hurt more than she had expected.

He pulled her into his arms and tilted her chin up, forcing her to look at him. "I gave her away at the wedding," he said. "That counts for something, I hope."

"What do you mean?"

"Judging from that frown on your face, you don't approve. You think that maybe I led her on and then dumped her when she got too serious. But, Abby, I never lied to her and I never made any promises. I think that's why we're still friends. She married a guy I work with, somebody I introduced her to, incidentally."

Abby wasn't surprised. It was a smooth maneuver from a savvy but compassionate operator. That scenario could have come from a book on the most efficient and humane methods for dumping an old lover. She turned away, knowing she wasn't being fair. She'd just become too cynical. Better that, though, than playing the part of the trusting innocent. Never that again.

"You're frowning," he said.

Abby cleared her expression with an effort. "Sorry,

I suppose your story hit a nerve. My ex-husband tried to set me up with his best friend.''

Matt winced. ''Before or after the divorce?''

''During. He meant well, but it was not one of his better ideas,''she said with a rueful smile. ''Call Pop, will you? If we don't eat pretty soon, everything will be cold.''

''Except the bread,'' he reminded her.

''The bread? Oh, right.'' She dashed over to the oven and rescued the foil-wrapped loaf while Matt went in search of her father. By the time the two men returned, most of the food was on the table and the sauce was reheating in the microwave.

''About time,'' Pop muttered, coming through the doorway. ''A man could starve around here waiting for the two of you.'' He settled into his place and solemnly spread a plaid napkin in his lap.

Abby retrieved the sauce and quickly ladled it into a serving bowl. She simultaneously set it on the table and slid into her seat while her father waited expectantly. Then he bowed his head.

''Please bless this food, Lord. Amen.''

Short and to the point, typically Pop, she thought as she straightened and reached for the bread. She glanced across the table and caught Matt's gaze on her, unaccountably solemn.

''Did I forget something?'' Something important if his expression was any gauge.

Matt shook his head. ''It's this house. Even with just the three of us here it seems full, like the rest of the family might walk in at any minute, your sisters, the kids, even a cat or two.''

Pop passed the bowl of pasta to Matt. ''They just might,'' he said. ''So you'd better eat while there's still food in front of you.''

Matt's laugh was a low, wistful sound that caught at Abby's heart. She had a hunch there was much more to it than he'd admitted. He looked like a man who had spent too long on the outside pretending he didn't care what happened on the other side of the window.

"Jake Monroe, you're a lucky man," Matt said, looking pensive. "You have a lot to show for your life. Not everyone can say that."

Pop glanced up from the sauce, the ladle poised above his plate. "I have everything I need and almost everything I want."

Matt tilted his head at a thoughtful angle as he drew a deep breath, then let it out in a heavy sigh. "Your definition of success may be a lot better than mine has been. Money, it seems, doesn't make the kind of memories I sense in this house." He shook his head. "Imagine not wanting to leave home."

Abby shared a brief grin with her father. "Oh, we've all wanted to leave home and did it a few times. We keep coming back, though."

"Like I said, you're lucky."

Leaning forward, Pop spooned the sauce over his spaghetti and handed the bowl to Matt. "You know, I believe you really mean that. You're not bad for an East Coast city boy. What do you say we open that bottle Abby's been hiding in the refrigerator?"

She shoved back her chair. "That's what I forgot. The wine," she said, her voice slightly husky. It seems she wasn't the only one whose life hadn't taken the turns she'd expected. Matt had his own secrets. And his own regrets.

SEVEN

Abby didn't have a chance until much later to ask Matt why he'd become so pensive. Or maybe the question was, what did her family have that his didn't? Perhaps it was none of her business. It might be too difficult for him to talk about. But they had to if she was ever to understand him.

She'd just stuck the last pan into the soapy dishwater when he ambled slowly back into the kitchen.

"Need help?" he asked.

She smiled and tossed him a dish towel. "You can dry what's in the rack. What's Pop doing?"

"Snoring. He was telling me about his roses. He got to the part about grafting the Bourbons, and he dozed off right in the middle of a sentence. Must have been the wine," he answered.

She chuckled. "I'm surprised you're still awake. My eyes start to glaze over after the first two minutes."

"It was interesting." He took the largest pan from the top of the stack on the sideboard and swiped at it with the towel.

"Oh, really?" she asked skeptically.

"Okay, you caught me. The intricacies of grafting aren't really my specialty," he said. "However, he had some tips on picking flowers for his daughter. He said yellow daylilies are your favorite. I wish I'd known."

"You discussed that with my father?"

"He's a great guy. I wish my own father was that easy to talk to."

Abby stared in surprise. "Easy? You must be talking about a different Jake Monroe. Pop's the original brick wall when he gets his mind set on something. And believe me, he does that more often than I want to think about." She'd battered against that brick wall quite a bit lately. Judging from how easily he'd accepted Matt, there would be several more rounds to the battle in the next few days. Already, she could see how Pop's mind worked, neatly slotting Matt into the son-in-law category.

The thought didn't make her as uneasy as it might have once. She cast a surreptitious glance in Matt's direction. He dried the saucepan with quick, efficient movements, doing that as neatly as everything else he did.

He looked up, catching her stare. "Aren't I doing it right?"

She smiled nervously. "Can I ask you something personal?"

"Ask me anything," he said. "For you, my life is an open book."

"I wonder." She shut off the stream of water, then turned, leaning back against the sink and crossing her arms.

"Oh, no—" He smacked his free hand against his forehead. "You found out about the other wives."

The tired old line broke through Abby's seriousness,

eliciting a dry laugh. "Certainly not from you. Matt, why don't you talk about your family?"

Comprehension dawned in his expression like the lights coming on along the midway at dusk. He nodded slowly, setting the pan aside. "I see. Your father has welcomed me into your home, introduced me to your entire family, even the minister, too. You're wondering when you'll meet my family."

She released a frustrated breath that fluttered her bangs across her damp forehead. "This isn't the nineteen fifties, and I'm not a starry-eyed innocent counting the steps to the altar. Of course, I'd like to meet your family, when and if you want to introduce us."

"Are you sure?" he asked, his expression closed though his voice carried a teasing note. "For all you know, my father could be in prison and my mother an ax-murderer."

"Could be where you acquired your business skills," she retorted. "I've heard you referred to as the ax-man more than once. But that's beside the point."

"What is the point?"

"You obviously think I'm prying," she said. "I don't mean to. You can tell me to shut up and mind my own business. It's just that you've said some surprising things today, some things I don't understand. All that stuff about how lucky Pop is. You sounded as if you envy him. Or is that just a show to ingratiate yourself with my father?"

Matt looked down at his hands, twisting the striped dish towel in a spiral, then let it unwind in slow circles. "It's not a bad idea, but I didn't think of it."

"I'm not surprised. You've never struck me as a family man. Yet there you were getting soft-eyed with my father over a bottle of Chianti. You've severely damaged your image as a corporate tough guy."

Matt met her gaze steadily, though his expression told her little. "Let's just say that your father's life has layers that mine never will. I envy him that, and I envy you and your sisters. My childhood wasn't filled with laughter and cozy family get-togethers. Most of the relatives couldn't deal with my sister's problems, especially the seizures. She took up so much of Mom and Dad's time that they didn't have a whole lot left over for me. After she died, there was too much time. We couldn't talk. We couldn't even look at each other. We went our separate ways, like three robots living in the same house and pretending we were fine."

Abby watched him, trying to imagine it. But she couldn't. The Monroes had always leaned on one another and propped one another up, laughed and cried together. Emotional isolation was outside her experience.

"Anyway," he continued. "I grew up pretty fast, got myself in some trouble, and grew up some more."

"What kind of trouble?"

He shrugged. "That's another story. Now, I am who I am. My parents retired to Florida, have inane hobbies, and are pretty much happy. We talk once in a while, but I don't feel that close to them, not like you and your father."

Abby had to laugh. "Maybe you should consider yourself blessed," she said. "Pop can be a real pain."

Matt started to protest. Then he must have noticed her skepticism. "I had noticed a few strong hints about my intentions toward you," he admitted.

She felt a moment's panic, then quickly pushed it away. Pop might hint about matrimony, but he wouldn't tell her secrets. "I'm sorry. He's been doing that since I was sixteen." She shrugged dismissively and turned back to the sink to empty the dishpan. "He's from another generation."

"And your unmarried state upsets the natural order," Matt finished for her.

She grinned over her shoulder. "Worse. I'm a divorcée with no immediate prospects or inclination to correct the situation."

It was Matt's turn to stare at the ceiling. "You are a trial, Abby Monroe." His head slowly lowered, his expression a picture of puzzlement as he repeated her name. "What was your husband's name?"

"Tom Bradford. Why?" She stowed the dishpan under the sink and dried her hands.

"Your name," he said by way of explanation.

"Oh, I see. I never took his last name. Pop blames my streak of feminist stubbornness. His words, not mine."

"I'll bet you had separate checking accounts." Matt snapped the towel at her. "You probably even refused to say 'obey' in the marriage ceremony."

She laughed and tossed him another towel. "Damn right."

"What happened?"

She hesitated, then grabbed her own towel.

"Sorry, you don't have to answer that."

"It's no secret. I met Tom when I was still in college. It was the grand passion I thought I'd been waiting for. But he liked to walk on the edge. I like it safe. We decided to go our separate ways before we ruined what was left of our friendship."

Matt watched her carefully. "So it was an amicable divorce."

"Mostly. We managed to stay friends."

"Is he the reason you're so careful around me? Do you still have feelings for him?"

"Are you asking if I'm still in love with my ex-husband?"

He lifted his chin. "Yes, I guess that is what I'm asking."

She shook her head. "I'll always love Tommy. I'm not sure I ever was really in love with him, not the way I should have been. It takes more than sex to make a good marriage."

"So I hear." Matt accepted her frank explanation with matter-of-fact calm. He shook out his towel, then picked up another pan. "What's he doing now?"

Abby froze, startled by his question. "I guess I never told you. Tommy's dead."

Matt looked uncomfortable. "I'm sorry."

"It's okay. He died the way he lived, on the edge and probably having the time of his life until the tire blew. Matt, my ex-husband died a year after the divorce on a dirt track in Oklahoma. If it hadn't been then and there, it would have been someplace else. I never really understood that wild streak in him.

"Now here's a clean towel," she said, handing him one. "Quit stalling and get busy. He only sleeps for a half hour or so. If we hurry, we can get finished here and slip out for a walk. It'll save you from the rest of the grafting lesson."

"Good idea," Matt said. "This is probably the last lazy day I'll get for a while."

She opened the bottom cabinet and began stowing the dried pans and utensils. "You're thinking about the park again, aren't you?"

She heard him come up behind her, and she reached for the pan he held out. He clenched it tightly for a moment until she looked at him, a question in her eyes. "I came to this city because of AmericaLand," he told her. "And it gave me an excuse to stay. I just hope that business won't take up too much of my time."

She let a slow, sultry smile curve her lips as she took

the pan from his relaxed grip. "That makes two of us," she admitted, her voice slightly husky.

News of Brett Holland's official departure from AmericaLand spread quickly. Though Abby sensed some trepidation afoot about the park's future, word filtered down from the department heads that no layoffs or firings were planned this season. So on the surface, it soon became business as usual. She felt as if she and Matt were back to the cat and mouse game, passing in corridors, surprising one another at odd moments, leaving notes and telephone messages.

Then he instituted an aggressive advertising campaign, along with ticket specials, to bring in the crowds and shore up the park's attendance figures. At the same time, he brought in an outside accounting firm for an exhaustive audit of company records.

Abby didn't know whether to be relieved or exasperated by the entire situation. On the one hand, the walkways became crowded with fun-seekers. Supplies were readily available, and maintenance work was almost on schedule, thanks to the additional hirings Matt authorized. On the other, supervising the rejuvenation consumed so much of his time that she didn't see him except in passing or over hastily grabbed sandwiches. After nearly two weeks of telephone tag and interrupted meals, Abby had had enough.

"Are you sure he's still here?" she asked Bethany as she peeked in her office door. The building was mostly dark, with light showing under only a couple of doors besides her sister's.

"Positive," Bethany replied, looking up from the stack of papers. "He's in the conference room waiting for these figures from the advertising agency. Want to take them in for me?"

"Is it urgent?"

Bethany sighed. "Not really, if you ask me. We can't act on anything until Monday, when the bank opens. That means we have all weekend to put the proposal together."

"Proposal?"

"Matt's putting together a new business plan. New financing. New promotions. New rides. Maybe even a concert hall to bring in some big-name acts. Just your normal stuff to keep the public from getting bored with us."

Abby took a step inside. "As in loud music and heart-thumping bass? I hear the concerts can be real money-makers for some of the other parks. Just make sure it's far away from the dolphins."

"That's not my department," Bethany argued, holding her hands up in a defensive pose. "Talk to Matt about any ideas you have. He's meeting with an architect tomorrow morning."

"I'll do that," Abby said, turning away. As long as he was thinking about renovations and new attractions, she had a few suggestions of her own.

"Wait a minute," Bethany called. "I saw the test kit in the bathroom wastebasket."

Abby leaned back through the doorway. "Shush. I don't want the whole world to know."

Bethany waved her hands in the air in exasperation. "There's nobody here except us."

"And Matt."

"He's at the other end of the building. Now what happened? Did the rabbit die?"

Abby shook her head slowly. "Not yet, though it's only been five days since the last time at the clinic. I'll try again in a few days."

"I'm sorry," Bethany said.

"It doesn't mean much yet. I just jumped the gun on the testing." She stepped closer. "I'll let you know when there's something to tell. Do you want me to take those papers in?"

"Yeah." Bethany handed over several sheets, grabbed her briefcase, and switched off the lights. "Give me a minute to get out of the building. If he has any questions, I'll be home tomorrow morning."

"Tough to work for, huh?" Abby suggested.

"A little demanding. Count to thirty before you take another step," Bethany ordered as she backed down the hall.

"Whatever." Abby leaned against the wall until Bethany turned the corner. Then she headed for the conference room, whistling the Ferris wheel calliope tune. The sound echoed merrily in the emptiness, in time with the soft sound of her footsteps on the polished tiles.

Matt was leaning back in his chair, waiting expectantly when Abby strode through the doorway. His hair was rumpled, as if he'd combed restless fingers through it more than once while he pored over the stacks of papers scattered across the table. He looked tired but glad to see her.

"You sound happy. What's the occasion?" he asked.

"I heard an interesting rumor a while ago," she told him. "I thought maybe we could discuss it over dinner." She dropped Bethany's papers in front of him, then tugged him out of the chair. "Don't tell me you've eaten already because I checked up on you."

"I've been waiting for you," he said, glancing at his watch. "Don't you have another show yet tonight?"

She shook her head. "Nope. This is Jay's weekend to work late. Can you spare me an hour?"

He sighed, a tired smile touching his lips. "I need a

break, and I need food. Do you want to call out for sandwiches again?''

She grinned. ''I thought you might enjoy a change of pace tonight.''

''Pizza?''

''In here?'' she said. ''Sounds boring.''

''Quiet and private.'' He reached for her, but she skipped out of his reach.

''Come with me. I have a surprise for you. Leave the tie here. You won't be needing it.'' She paused in the doorway, her fingers tapping restlessly against the gray metal frame while she watched him. He loosened the tie with short, jerky motions. He then tossed it across the papers she'd brought him.

''Where to?'' he asked, following her down the hallway toward the side exit.

''Someplace I doubt you've been before.''

He glanced at her, his expression uncertain in the bright light mounted over the door. ''Are you speaking in double entendres, or have I just been working too many late nights alone?''

''You've definitely spent too much time working to be expected to think clearly at this time of night. We're having a picnic.'' She ran a tantalizing finger along the line of his chin and smiled. ''A private picnic. To talk business.''

He nodded. ''Business. Right.'' He took her hand, lacing his fingers between hers, then began to whistle the calliope tune.

''You're not half bad at that,'' she said. ''You should enter the talent show.''

''What talent show?''

''In August. It's usually the last Saturday night before school starts. The employees stay late.''

''Ride the rides. Party,'' Matt filled in.

"Partly. We have an untalent show, which is a showcase of unusual and generally useless talents. Remember Phil, the maintenance man?"

"How could I forget?"

"He plays the *William Tell Overture* on a carpenter's saw."

"Oh, really?" He sounded skeptical.

"Yes, really. He's not bad either."

Matt smiled down at her. "I never would have taken him for a classical music fan."

Abby laughed, feeling the excitement of his nearness mingle with the infectious revelry of the crowd as they slipped into the French Quarter. A starburst of fireworks flared overhead, showering the night sky with sparks.

"You know, not everything Brett did was wrong," she said. "The employee night is a good tradition. I hope you don't intend to cancel it this year."

"That would be a little hard on morale. Besides, I can't imagine it costing that much."

"Free food," she answered.

Matt looked startled. "For three thousand employees?"

"And their guests. But not everyone comes. Don't forget, it doesn't start until one A.M."

He groaned. "I don't have to come, do I?"

"A token appearance would suffice. Come on. This way," Abby said, pulling him off the path. They cut around the rear of the Bourbon Street Café and into the kitchen.

"Hey, Marty. Got that basket ready?" she called over the sizzle of the fryer.

"Right there on the counter behind you," a thin-faced girl with an oversized apron said.

"Thanks, I owe you," Abby said. She handed the basket to Matt, then slipped out the door.

"Follow me," she instructed. She led the way around

two overstuffed dumpsters and along the fence that rimmed the back edge of the Bourbon Street strip of shops. At the end, she tested a series of boards until she found the loose one.

"I'll put in a repair order," he said as she swung the wide plank out of the way.

"Don't you dare. This is another long-standing tradition known only to us old-timers." She took the basket from him and stood back while he shimmied through the narrow opening. She pulled a flashlight from the top of the basket and shone it on the ground while she picked her way through the shadowy undergrowth of the trees.

"Where are we going?"

"Hush up and watch your step," she said. "It's been a long time since anyone cleared the brush in this part of the woods."

A moment later, they crossed under the high curve of the Speedroller and back into the shadows. "Almost there," she said, shining the light onto a trio of thick oaks. Beneath the dark canopy of leaves stood a picnic table.

"How long has this been here?"

"As long as I've worked here. Jay and I repainted it last summer."

Matt took the flashlight from her, flicking it off. "There's enough moonlight here. No sense in running the batteries down."

Abby looked skeptically around her. The moonlight shone in the open space around the Speedroller. Right here, they stood in the shadows beneath the trees. "Makeout Corner." That's what this place was called when she first came here. An apt name for a likely place, if you didn't mind being interrupted by teenagers who wanted to share the spot, she decided.

"Tell me about your new business plan," she prompted. "Bethany says you're considering a concert hall." She spread the contents of the basket across the table while she talked.

"It's one of the suggestions on the list."

"Not bad, if you give us a seal pool, too." She handed him a spoon and a covered Styrofoam bowl. He popped off the lid and dipped a finger inside to taste it.

"Mmm. Not bad for reconstituted gumbo," he said.

"You're not answering the question."

"What would it cost?"

"The numbers are your department, not mine. Basically, we'd need a duplicate of what we have now for the dolphins, minus the seating. One performance arena would do, but the seals and dolphins have to be penned separately. They don't get along that well."

"You're talking about a lot of money."

She shrugged in the darkness. "Not as much as a whole new concert hall, I'd bet. I'm not sure how much Marine Shows charges for the seals contract, but you probably wouldn't need another trainer or more ushers. There would just be the additional water, pool maintenance, and so forth."

"Have you worked with seals before?" Matt's hand closed over hers.

Abby pulled her hand away and rummaged around in the picnic basket, searching for the box of crullers she'd ordered. "I've worked with them enough to know that they're real crowd pleasers. Anyway, it's just a suggestion. The seals are popular, though."

He leaned across the table, watching her thoughtfully. Her eyes had adjusted enough for her to see his expression more clearly in the darkness. "You could put together a proposal," he said.

"That would be inappropriate," she countered. "I'm not an AmericaLand employee."

"You and your company could benefit from any changes."

"Possibly. That's assuming that Marine Shows puts in a bid and that AmericaLand doesn't decide to go with another firm," she replied.

"You could have the inside advantage."

"You could always check with the Panama City office. I'm sure someone there has a pretty good idea of current costs. It would be enough for an estimate, wouldn't it?"

"I'll put it on the list. And now, I have a favor to ask of you."

"What's that?" She broke off a cruller, popping one end into her mouth and the other into his. His lips closed around her finger, warm and moist as he sucked the powdered sugar from it. He kissed the fingertip, then let her pull away.

"I need a big favor. A date for a very formal and probably very boring reception."

"Sure. When is it?"

Matt hesitated, wincing slightly. "Tomorrow night. I know it's short notice, but I didn't find out about it until this morning. It's a fund-raiser or something like that. The invitation was buried in Brett's papers."

"That's okay. Just because none of your other women could go . . ." she teased, letting the words trail off into light laughter. Then she saw the look on his face and the laughter faded into a wave of warmth that flowed through her like a hot summer wind.

"I don't have any other women," he said, his voice low and sincere.

Abby tilted her head sideways, watching him for a

moment. Then she rose on tiptoe and leaned across the table to kiss him lightly. "I like that."

He cupped her face with gentle hands. His lips touched hers again with whispering tenderness that promised instead of demanded. She answered with every stirring emotion floating through her. Something as sweet as first love but more knowing welled up in her, mingling the physical sensations of his touch with needs of her heart. She touched him, too, teasing with restless fingers until he groaned. He brushed aside the picnic clutter with a single sweep of his arm, then stepped onto the seat, across the tabletop, and down onto her side of the bench. He leaped to the ground and reached for her, swinging her up into his arms. Her hands automatically curled around his neck, securing her position.

"What are you doing?" she asked, giggling.

"Acting on my instincts," he replied. "Do you mind?"

She nibbled playfully along his neck. "Not a bit," she whispered.

"Prove it," he challenged.

"This doesn't prove it?" She kissed the pulse at the base of his neck. She drew a deep breath, savoring the warm male scent of his cologne mingling with the woodsy smells around them. Earthy smells. Elemental smells that ignited basic instincts that made her body burn with its own inner heat. Her fingers stroked the curling hairs at his collar, then laced through the thickness at the crown of his head, easing his lips gently closer.

His eyes darkened to deep black pools before his lids sank closed, hiding the yearning. Abby felt a thrill of womanly power as she stroked his temples. His skin felt warm beneath her fingertips and surprisingly soft.

The last evidence of the tense lines faded into tenderness as fragile as her own heart and as easily damaged. Her own eyelids became too heavy to hold open as he kissed her again. Still clinging to her, he leaned back, sinking to the picnic bench, his arms tightening about her. She was so close she could feel his heart beating against her breast in an echo of her own thudding pulse.

But it wasn't enough. She needed to touch him. Without thinking, she undid his top button, then another, and kissed the firm flesh beneath the starched cotton. While her lips tasted him, her hands were busy, pulling the shirt free of his waistband and stealing up the smooth expanse of his back. She felt the powerful flex of his muscles as he hauled her up against him.

"I could make love to you right here, right now, on top of this picnic table," he whispered as he slipped his hands up under her shirt.

She looked up into his face. Smoky desire stared back at her, stealing her breath. She closed her eyes, then gasped as he skimmed along the underside of her breasts with feather lightness.

She caught at his forearms, feeling the subtle movements of bone and muscle as his fingers splayed across her breasts, cupping them beneath the loose shirt.

"Making love is something I take very seriously," she warned him.

"Me, too." His eyes trapped hers, holding her still while the tingling sensations sparked through her. "I want you very much. But I want more than a quick lay with splinters in your back, mosquito bites on mine, and a hundred screaming teenagers on the roller coaster behind us."

Abby drew a deep breath, trying to hold her thoughts while his stroking fingers steadily coaxed them away. "Sounds interesting, and altogether too tempting,'' she said, then tightened her fingers on his arms. ''But I wasn't talking about time and place, Matt. It's been a very long time since I let a man touch me this way.''

''How long?''

''Years. Since before the divorce.'' Making love was a sacred trust between a man and a woman, at least that's the way it should be, she thought.

''But there have been temptations?''

''None this strong,'' she admitted.

''You were made to be touched this way. I suppose you've been told that before.'' His thumbs brushed across her nipples, moving in slow, tantalizing circles.

''It's not exactly an original line,'' she replied.

''It's the truth.'' His hands slid downward to grasp her waist. He kissed her again, long and hard until she could barely breathe. And when he raised his head, his own breathing was harsh and ragged.

She slid her hands along his shoulders to caress his neck, then reverently touch his face. ''I feel like a teenager again, but I can't act like one. I have definite plans, things I want too badly to set aside any longer. I'm too old to play games with chance. I'm not sure where you fit into my life.'' Abby drew a deep breath as she searched his face in the darkness. ''Or where you want to fit in,'' she added after a moment.

''What do you want from life?''

Abby watched him steadily. ''What everyone else wants, happiness, someone to love, children, satisfying work.''

He held her close, hugging her tightly against him. ''I need you. As much as I want to make love to you, I think I need your warmth, your friendship even more. I don't want to risk that.''

Abby cupped his face in her hands, raising on tiptoe to kiss him. "I don't think you could."

"Be very, very sure," he said. "Friends are more precious than lovers. I'd walk away before I'd damage what we have already."

And with those words, Abby tipped over the precipice and into love with Matt Gardner.

EIGHT

Abby felt exposed in the borrowed strapless dress with its high slit and short skirt. She never should have let Bethany talk her into trying it on, let alone wearing it tonight to this brightly lit ballroom full of people. Only politeness to her present companions kept her from slipping away to the ladies' room again to tug the black brocade bodice higher over her bare skin. That and the electric heat arcing between her and Matt all evening.

When he first saw her, he'd looked as though he wanted to back her into a closet and take the dress off. And when they'd reached the car, he'd said so. Just the memory brought a naughty smile to her lips—lips still swollen from kisses that hadn't just smudged her lipstick but erased every trace of it. Yes, she felt exposed. And vulnerable. And completely out of her element in more ways than she cared to consider. She ran her finger around the rim of the glass and forced her attention back to the present.

"Mrs. Palmer, I think the auction went well, don't

you?" she told the woman next to her. The man who made the introductions earlier insisted the gray-haired matriarch was a driving force behind tonight's fund-raiser for Children's Mercy Hospital.

The woman smiled, though her eyes assessed Abby as shrewdly as any business owner reviews a balance sheet. "Just wonderfully, Abby. It is Abby, isn't it? From the theme park. You work with the porpoises. That must be interesting."

"It has its rewards, though entertainment isn't nearly as noble as the work you're doing. I've heard the money raised tonight set a new record."

"It's nearly enough to pay for the equipment in the oncology wing. Now we just need a few volunteers to help in the wards."

"Are you hinting?"

"Of course. You do have spare time, don't you?"

Abby parried with a wide, wary smile. "Precious little, though I could post a few notices in prominent places at the park." Time, or the lack of it, wasn't the problem, though she didn't care to share that with Mrs. Palmer. At any other point in her life, she'd have dived into the project. Now, though, she knew she had to be careful to avoid exposure to some of the more damaging viruses afoot in a children's ward, viruses that wouldn't hurt her much but could prove damaging to a developing fetus.

She smiled, trying to cover her guilt over her selfishness. "Some of our performers might be willing to put on a show for the children. My dolphins, I'm afraid, won't be able to attend unless you've recently installed a very, very large swimming pool," she teased.

"Something for next year's auction?" Mrs. Palmer's eyes glinted with pleasure as she crooked her arm through Abby's, leading her gently across the room. "Come along now, dear. You can help me convince a few more people to part with their hoarded cash. You distract them with that dress and those legs and I'll pick their pockets. You know, I had nice legs once."

"Somehow, I don't think you needed them to get what you want," Abby replied dryly.

"A smart woman chooses the method that works best, be it her brains, her body, or her bank account," Mrs. Palmer said.

While they walked, Abby glanced around, searching idly for Matt. She'd seen him by the piano earlier, talking to a group of business types dressed in almost matching tuxedos. He wasn't there now, though.

"Have you met the mayor?" Mrs. Palmer asked, stopping halfway across the room. She made the introductions, then moved on, leaving Abby to fend for herself. She spent the next five minutes talking politics and answering questions about porpoises. Then she spotted Matt nearby, deep in conversation with a banker she recognized from a newspaper photograph, She set her glass in the base of a handily placed potted plant and headed in their direction.

"There you are," Matt said, breaking off as she approached. His intimate smile reminded her of their kiss earlier that evening, and she felt herself flush with remembered pleasure. She slipped her hand into his, squeezing lightly.

"If I'm interrupting, I'll mingle a while longer," she said, flashing a quick look at the banker.

"Not at all," Matt insisted. "Mr. Mason, have you met my very good friend, Abby Monroe?"

The older man's knowing expression indicated he'd branded her with his definition for blond female friends, and she felt an immediate dislike for the man. "Your reputation has preceded you, Mr. Mason,'' she answered, pitting her cool gaze against his sly smile.

''You mustn't believe everything you read,'' he replied, looking amused. ''Matthew, I'd like to talk with you more on Monday. Do you have any free time in the afternoon?''

Matt smiled. ''I believe so. I'll have my secretary call you and arrange something,'' he said.

''Good, good. And now, I suppose I'd better find my wife before Liza Palmer talks her into donating anything else.''

''She is quite persuasive, isn't she?'' Abby said.

''The woman's dangerously good at her work,'' the banker agreed. ''I'd hire her myself, but she'd end up stealing my job.'' He shook Matt's hand, then disappeared into the crowd.

''I think we've been here long enough, don't you?'' Matt said when Mr. Mason was gone.

''Yes, my very good friend,'' she replied with a sarcastic grin. ''Mr. Mason put his own interpretation on that wonderful little introduction.''

''I hope you are my very good friend.''

She rolled her eyes toward the glittering conical chandelier. ''By whose definition?''

Matt shrugged. ''He's a dirty old man. But his bank might finance some of the changes I'm considering.''

''So he's a useful dirty old man. Enough business for tonight. I'd give just about anything to get out of these shoes,'' she said, beginning to work her way toward the wide ballroom doors.

''They do look a bit lethal. I could carry you, spare your poor feet the agony of walking. And the view would be pretty good from that angle.'' A devilish twinkle sparked in his eyes as he leaned closer, sidestepping a waiter laden with a tray of used glasses.

Abby noticed the direction of his gaze, which had slipped to the low-cut bodice that revealed more than it concealed. "I'll manage, thank you."

"It would give them something to talk about tomorrow," he said.

"Mm. Free publicity," she mused, a mildly sarcastic tone underlying her words. "That should help your expansion project."

He squeezed her hand. "Chicken," he accused.

They'd nearly reached the lobby when someone hailed Matt. He turned, hiding his annoyance behind a questioning smile. "I'm sorry, have we met?" he asked the man who approached. Stoutly muscular, the man had a bulldog face that looked vaguely familiar. She realized he'd been across the table from her at dinner.

"Sam Thompson, isn't it?" she said.

"Yes, I'm an architect with Bracale, Kasper & Steward. We're in the Weston Building," he said, handing over a business card.

"I mentioned earlier that you might be interviewing architects for the preliminary plans soon," Abby said. "I hope you don't mind. Mr. Thompson has been involved in some projects at the zoo."

"At the zoo, huh?" Matt cast a knowing glance her way. "You definitely are angling for that new seal pool."

She raised her chin slightly. "Actually, a renovation of the entire complex would be in order."

His pupils widened perceptively, and she wondered if she'd said too much that should have been kept private. After all, they'd barely discussed this, and she'd all but opted out of any involvement. But then this opportunity had presented itself, and she was never one to overlook an opportunity.

"You did suggest I work on the proposal," she countered. "Maybe you'd have a little time on Monday morning to discuss some of your ideas, say before my ten thirty show? Is that convenient for you, Mr. Thompson?" She turned to the architect, who had been watching them with increasing discomfort.

"Mr. Gardner?" he said, his tone uncertain.

Matt considered a moment. "I have a couple of interviews next week. I think one is with a senior partner in your firm. Was he involved in the zoo project?"

"No, sir. I believe he was working in Saudi Arabia at the time. He specializes in large commercial projects."

"Perhaps you should sit in on the interview," Matt suggested. "Abby has raised some concerns particular to the aquatic mammals. You seem better equipped to handle that aspect than your associate."

A careful smile crossed the architect's face. "I don't believe I'd better suggest that to him, though I will tell him I spoke with you tonight."

Matt grinned, then shook hands easily with the man. "Please do. I'm interested in hearing your suggestions." The man murmured his good-byes and ambled back in the direction of the ballroom. Matt watched him for a moment, a frown overtaking his expression.

"Are you angry?" she asked quietly as they turned toward the lobby again.

"Because you took a little initiative? I did ask for your help," he said. "And that man could prove to be the genius I'm looking for."

"In an unlikely package," Abby commented, then immediately regretted it. "I'm sorry. That was tacky."

"He does have the look of a sumo wrestler dropout, don't you think?"

She had to laugh. "You don't think I overstepped my bounds?"

"I'm not Brett Holland. I don't have his kind of ego

problems or his power kicks. I don't care who makes the process work, just that it works well," he said. She stole a sidelong glance in his direction. He stared straight ahead, looking slightly annoyed.

"Your modesty overwhelms me," she said, hoping to tease the irritation out of him.

"Oh, I'm not modest. I know who I am and what I can do. And I appreciate anybody else with a reasonable combination of confidence and ability." He stopped, casually taking both her hands. "It's what first attracted me to you."

She tilted her head, reading the tenderness behind his unwavering gaze. "I thought it was the challenge."

He shook his head. "You're different, unpredictable, and exciting. I never know what to expect."

She smiled. "Neither do I. From you or from myself these days." She pulled away and stepped into the revolving door. She wasn't sure what came next. It didn't matter. She was enjoying the ride too much to get out a road map and try to figure out exactly where she was and where she was headed. Tonight, she simply intended to enjoy herself and let the future take care of itself for once.

Outside, the Saturday night sounds of a downtown still alive with city sounds filled her ears. So she felt rather than heard Matt as he came up behind her. He handed his claim slip to the valet in the long black coat that looked uncomfortable in this hot, muggy weather.

"You know, I've grown accustomed to the odd hours at the park already," Matt commented as he glanced at his watch. "Ten o'clock seems early."

"Same here. We could go to the Tuba. They have a great blues band on Saturday nights." Nothing but an inquisitive father and a second pregnancy test awaited her at home, and it probably was still too soon for an accurate reading.

He was shaking his head. "Not the Tuba. It's too crowded. Too much noise."

"How about a movie?"

He glanced down at his dark clothes, with the knife-pleat trousers and expensive silk shirt. "Dressed like this?"

"Why not?"

"I can think of about a dozen reasons," he replied, grinning broadly. He stood in silence, rocking heel to toe until Abby had to laugh.

"You really don't want to see a movie, do you?" she said. His quick leer said he had other things in mind. He leaned closer, his breath whispering against her neck when he spoke.

"It might be a lot more fun to drive out to the lake and look at the stars. Maybe try out the picnic tables there."

"That sounds interesting." She glanced up at the narrow corridor of night sky between the tall buildings. Bright pin dots of light dusted the moonless black space, making her want to leave the city noise and distractions behind for a while. There was something seductive about an evening under the stars, with nothing but crickets and bullfrogs for background music. And bugs.

"Mosquitoes," she reminded him. Reality was so much less romantic than the imagination.

He sighed loudly. "Right. Let's hit the movies. We can neck in the back and embarrass all the teenagers." He stepped off the curb as his car rounded the corner and eased under the wide hotel awning. They picked up a newspaper from a vending machine and spent the next five minutes arguing about which movie to see.

Abby lifted the paper, trying to read the showing times in the fine print by the dim visor light. "There's always the *Rocky Horror Picture Show*. But we'll have to wait until midnight."

"Not our crowd anymore," he said.

"Speak for yourself, Grandpa."

He shot her a warning look, then reached for the paper. "Wait a second. Let me see that."

"You drive, I'll read," she retorted. "I think we should head back out to Johnson County. Then we'll both be closer to home when the movie lets out."

"Check the article on the back side. It's something about meteors."

Abby refolded the page and held it up to the tiny light. "Meteor showers tonight," she summarized, then read the brief article aloud. She leaned back against the seat. "When I was a little girl, we used to spread our sleeping bags on the driveway and lie there, counting the shooting stars until we fell asleep."

"On the hard concrete?"

She shrugged in the darkness. "We were kids. We didn't really notice."

"What about the mosquitoes?"

"We didn't notice them, either. Damn the mosquitoes. Let's go watch the stars. We could stop by my house and pick up some bug repellent," she coaxed. She'd much rather be alone with Matt than share him with a theater full of people.

"Or we could go back to my place." He waggled his eyebrows in an exaggerated leer.

"What do you take me for? A cheap fool?"

He chuckled. "All right. There's a 400 mm telescope in the den of my apartment. We could pick it up on the way."

"That sounds perfect." She buckled her seat belt and

settled back for the ride. "Where is your apartment, anyway?"

"It's a townhouse in a brick and stone complex just off I-35, south of the park," he said.

Her eyebrows rose in the dark. "Nice." That was an understatement. She and Bethany had done some halfhearted apartment hunting before Mom got sick. They'd seen the price tag for condos in that complex, gasped, and moved on to less expensive listings.

"It's not bad, though I don't spend much time there," Matt said. "Since I'm subletting, it's already furnished with everything I need. All I had to do was stock the refrigerator."

"If Marine Shows provided a place like that, I wouldn't be living at home," Abby replied. "You should see Jay's apartment. Early seventies generic with thin walls and sunscreen scum in the pool."

Matt groaned. "Sounds awful. I guess I'm lucky I found this place."

"We make our own luck," she said. "That's my motto."

His hand caught hers. "I knew the minute I saw you that we had a lot in common."

"Yeah, we're both older than ninety-five percent of the employees at the park," she taunted.

They traded lighthearted barbs for the rest of the way. It wasn't until he stopped the car in front of a two-story row of residences that Abby fell into awed silence. The brick and stone edifice appeared solid and imposing behind the landscaped shrubbery and flagstone walks.

"Which one is it?" she asked after a moment.

"The one with the daylilies blooming by the steps," he said as they climbed out.

"You do have a thing about daylilies, don't you?" she retorted.

"Since a certain sunny July afternoon," he said. "I took one look at the front of this place and said I'd take it." He jingled his keys all the way to the door.

"Without waiting to see the inside," Abby pressed. "Not a chance. You wouldn't risk the possibility of pet odors, bad pipes, or sagging floors."

"Not to mention ugly wallpaper," Matt answered. The door swung open, revealing a paved path of brick-red tile leading gallery style through the townhouse.

She stepped into the air-conditioned interior and glanced around. Natural wood tones against nubby carpeting and furniture cushions of warm browns and reds lent an overall feeling of comfort. Then her eyes began to pick out the details, the soapstone woodstove in the corner, the carved totems arranged in a row on the antique sled that doubled as a coffee table. And the telescope placed strategically next to a wide window with a surprisingly unobstructed view of the ribbon of highway leading toward the downtown skyline.

"*This* is why you took the place," she said, spinning around.

He shook his head. "It was the daylilies," he insisted. "Make yourself at home. There's some soda in the fridge, even a bottle of wine if you're feeling adventurous."

"Wine, cheese, the stars. What more could a girl ask for?"

"Mosquito repellent," he retorted.

Abby made a face and sank into the thick cushions of the sofa. She heard the soft tap of his shoes on the tiles, then the squeak of a door. So the place wasn't perfect. The man who lived here now was as close to it as she'd found in her thirty-three years.

She kicked off her shoes and settled back, letting her eyelids droop closed as she thought about the last few weeks. And the weeks to come. The time was so short, just two months until autumn. So little time and so much to find out about one another, so much she had to know. Whether he could learn to love her, whether he might someday want children, whether he could accept that she couldn't wait until someday arrived and had taken matters into her own hands. Whether he made love as magnificently as he kissed.

A noise from the gallery broke through her thoughts. She blinked, turning her head ever so slightly. Matt stood in sock feet on the tiles, watching her with an odd, almost possessive expression on his face.

"Matt?"

He cleared his throat. "I wondered . . ." he said hoarsely, his voice trailing off. "Never mind, I'll be ready in a minute." He turned and disappeared behind the squeaking door again.

What had he intended to say? She drew a deep breath, then rose to her feet. She didn't want to drive out to the lake to look at the stars. And she would bet he didn't, either. She padded quietly to the door, then pushed it open, barely noticing the noise of the hinge this time.

He sat on the bed, his hands dangling between his knees. His eyes clenched closed, then opened as she approached.

"What's wrong, Matt?"

He stiffened. "I'll be ready in a minute, as soon as I put on my shoes."

"You don't need your shoes," Abby said, suddenly sure of herself.

He didn't answer, didn't even move for a moment. He simply watched her, with tiger eyes that both frightened and drew her. "You shouldn't be in here," he whispered.

"Maybe not, but I want to be."

"What about the stars?"

"I don't need them. Do you?" She moved closer, stopping bare inches from him. Then she took a single, deliberate step into the open circle of his arms. She stood there a moment, staring down with steady sureness.

"And your dreams?" he pressed. "You can't stay in this room and keep things as they are."

A wide smile of anticipation crossed her face. "Maybe this next step is part of the dream," she said. "I just didn't understand it until now."

He reached up and spanned her hips with slow, deliberate movements. Then, unexpectedly, he pulled her back onto the bed on top of him. She landed hard on his chest, giggling with surprise. He caught her wrists and stretched her arms out until she was lying on his chest, sprawled nose to nose with the man she loved. Lower, she could feel his hardness against her through the layers of cloth. A wild sense of exhilaration made her reckless. She wriggled against him, then lifted her head and licked her bottom lip.

Appreciative fire leaped in his eyes. "Excuse me, Ms. Monroe, but are you trying to seduce me?"

"Trying?" she responded playfully. "I must not be doing it right because I have every intention of seducing you tonight." She lowered her head, kissing a circle around his lips until he groaned in response. With one quick twist, he rolled them both over, reversing their positions.

Still pinning her wrists against the mattress, he lowered himself slowly, letting her absorb the weight of him, the male hardness against her softer flesh.

"Make absolutely sure this is what you want," he warned. "Make sure before this goes too far for either of us to stop. Plan on spending the entire night here, because it will take that and more for me to show you exactly how much I want you."

"Promises, promises," she whispered. "All I get is talk and promises."

"You're mine," he said, dipping his head to kiss her briefly before he spoke again, his tone trembling with emotion. "Whatever your plans are, tonight you belong to me."

His words were as possessive as the blatant way he held her body motionless on the bed. She was physically under his control. Yet she didn't feel the least bit trapped. He wouldn't hurt her, wouldn't do anything she didn't want him to do. And if she changed her mind, she could trust him to do as she wished.

Trust. The word echoed through her mind as his lips touched hers again. Trust. A whisper of faith riding atop the wave of emotion his tender touch wrought.

His hands released her wrists to trace a tingling trail up the sensitive skin of her inner arm. Her fingers tangled in his hair, pulling his lips back to hers. She poured all her newfound love into the kiss. His tongue teased against her teeth until she answered each probing thrust with one of her own. Abby savored the heady pleasure of it until tenderness faded beneath rising passion.

Then he turned his attention to her bare throat, the smooth slope of her shoulders, the soft skin above the bodice of the black brocade dress. Her breasts swelled with desire, straining against the boned lining. The memories of his thumbs brushing the peaked nipples flashed through her mind, and she moaned with need.

She shifted, sliding to the side as she reached for the

top button of his shirt. Her trembling fingers slipped it free, then the second and the third until she could kiss the lightly furred expanse of chest. He caught her fingers and held them for a moment, watching her steadily with passion-glazed eyes.

"We have the entire night," he said. Slowly he rose to his knees, balancing above her. He eased backwards until he reached the foot of the bed, pulling her with him as he stood.

The nubby texture of the carpeting rubbed against her stockinged feet, soothing the tired ache. She registered the sensation absently, her mind on other things. It had been a long time since she'd found herself at this point, but her body hadn't forgotten the intimate dance. She slid one slender foot across the floor to nuzzle against his larger one.

"Turn around," he said.

Abby tilted her chin upwards, smiling as she pirouetted. His hands rested lightly on her shoulders while he kissed the nape of her neck. "This way," he said, propelling her with gentle pressure across the room toward a set of sliding glass doors she hadn't seen before.

"Outside?"

"Not exactly." He opened the door, then followed her into a small glassed-in room. The tiled floor felt cool beneath her feet, though the room itself was warm and humid. He touched a series of switches and a low-watt light came on, throwing golden light onto a bubbling sunken hot tub.

"Now you know why I *really* took this place," Matt said.

She turned, a naughty smile crossing her lips. "A bachelor pleasure palace."

"You don't like it?"

"I like it fine," she said, leaning into the circle of his arms. His fingertips skimmed once again around the edge of the bodice, hesitated, then neatly slid the zipper down the back. The fabric slackened, then fell away, sliding down to catch on her hips, then slip lower to pool around her ankles. She stood there, naked except for a pair of French-cut silk and lace panties and black pantyhose.

"I know garters and stockings are supposed to be the costume for seduction these days, but the slit in that skirt just went too high," she said.

He drew a ragged breath. "I noticed. I've been wondering all night what you had on under that dress. Watching you across the room, peeking at the slit every time you took a step. You made it a little hard to concentrate on business and public relations."

"Good." She undid the last two buttons of his shirt and pushed it off his shoulders. Matt didn't remain passive while she did so. His hands cupped her breasts, his thumbs brushing slow, sensual circles around her peaked nipples. He bent low, kissing a path from her chin to her throat, then lower until his tongue retraced the pattern of his thumbs. The circle closed in a thin spiral until he sucked gently on the swollen nub. Then he turned his attention to the other.

Abby swayed against him, clutching at his shoulders. His tongue still occupied at her breast, he slipped his thumbs beneath the elastic band of her pantyhose. He tugged the band lower, rolling the nylon over her hips and down her legs until she pulled away, giggling at his frustration with the struggle against the clinging hose.

Matt caught her, swinging her up into his arms. "I will not be defeated by pantyhose." He strode back into the bedroom, turning sideways to maneuver them both through the door. Once through, he took three more steps and tossed her onto the bed. She bounced, laughing in shocked surprise.

He grabbed the elastic band and tugged the pantyhose down, pulling on the stretchy nylon until it slid over her ankles and popped off her feet. "Aha!" he yelled, then fell forward, landing on his outstretched arms.

"You won," Abby said, her voice low and husky.

He lowered himself, teasing her bare breasts with the light brush of his chest. "The mighty warrior," he said. His lips twitched as he collapsed in laughter, rolling over and pulling her on top of him.

She laughed along with him, feeling the exhilaration of shared anticipation, of the ridiculousness of his comment. Then the laughter died as her breathing quickened, as she felt the peaking arousal of her senses, of every fiber of her body.

She sat up, straddling his hips, then scooted lower, unbuckling his belt and sliding off the loose Dockers he'd just put on. His red cotton briefs swiftly followed. She climbed back onto the wide stripes of the puffed cotton comforter.

"I want you," she whispered. "I can't remember wanting anyone this much." She brushed her body against his, gasping when he caught her tightly against him. He held her a moment, then slid gentle hands along the curve of her spine. His touch sent heated waves of desire through her, steaming desire that stole her thoughts.

"I won't hurt you," he promised. "In any way. No unwelcome surprises as a result of tonight."

She tried to focus on his words, but it was difficult when his hands kept stroking such delicious trails along her skin. "Are you saying you won't make me pregnant? Don't worry, I've already taken care of that,'' she said, then giggled at the double entendre.

"And that's funny? Passion does strange things to you, Abby love." His hands slid lower, caressing her lower belly, then lower still.

"Maybe, it's just that—" She started to explain, but he cut her off with a devastating kiss. And still he caressed her, teasing her to the brink of madness with intuitive skill. She squirmed restlessly, grasping bunches of the bedspread in her clenched fists until he moved over her. She wrapped her legs around him, pulling him closer. And then he was inside her, filling her with mindless pleasure. She moved with him in age-old rhythm. And then she grabbed his shoulders, squeezing tightly as a thousand tiny stars burst behind her tightly clenched eyelids, filling her with shuddering ecstasy. Matt jerked, then trembled against her, whispering her name softly, over and over as he took her over the edge into a soaring world she'd never known.

Slowly, as the quivering sensations subsided, Abby became aware of small details. The comforting heat of Matt's skin against hers, the even sound of his breathing, the soft hum of the hot tub motor in the next room, the unbelievable satiated lassitude that almost numbed her limbs.

He rolled over, pulling her tightly against him. "I love you," he whispered.

She froze, wondering if she'd imagined those words. She lifted her head, studying his face. His eyes burned with intensity. He looked vulnerable and yet powerful at the same time.

"I love you, too," she said, her voice strong and sure. She stroked his temple, feeling empty and fulfilled at the same time. She affected him as deeply as he did her. And that frightened her. "I can't believe how much I love you. It came slowly, slipping up when I least expected it," she whispered.

He clenched her tightly against him, then eased the pressure as he sat up. He grasped both her hands and sat up, holding her gaze with his intensity.

"Then marry me," he said.

NINE

"Marry you?" Abby sat up slowly, unable to believe what she'd just heard. "You're serious, aren't you?"

Matt nodded, his warm brown eyes alight with love. He lifted her hands to his lips, kissing the knuckles. "Very, very serious," he assured her. "The two of us would make a great team."

Her mouth opened and closed twice, but no sound came out. She watched him for a moment in stunned silence. She hadn't come here with the intention of making love with him, at least not consciously. She supposed that underneath, everything had been leading in this direction, toward this bed. But marriage? She'd considered that, too, but her logic told her it was impossible. They came from two different places and were headed in different directions. They had simply paused at the crossroads of the X.

But her heart said something different. An incredulous smile stole onto her face. "Oh, Matt, I love you so much," she whispered.

"Then say you'll marry me." That heart-stopping

grin was back in place, and he leaned closer. "Tomorrow. Next week if you need time. Whenever you say."

"Slow down," she said. "It's been less than a month since we met."

He shrugged. "I know a good deal when I find it. I'm paid to make quick evaluations and act on them. Why can't I carry that into my private life?" Now he wore his boardroom look, that persuasive mien that preceded the big point designed to win her over. "I knew we'd be good together. And I was right."

Abby smiled. "You were right," she admitted.

"I usually am."

"But you don't have to marry me because we finally stopped dancing around in circles and made love. That's a pretty archaic tradition," she said.

He laughed. "You should know me better than that. I'm not an impetuous person. And I'm not so inexperienced that I'd mistake good sex for love. Do you think that's what this is about? I've known for weeks that I wanted to marry you. I knew it when you threw that jab at me about those flowers, how they only last a single day and then they shrivel up and die."

"So you brought me the beeswax ones," she said, remembering the fleeting expression she'd been unable to read the day he gave them to her. Now, she recognized it as the possessive yearning he wore now, only now he didn't try to hide it.

"I knew you were the woman I've been looking for, the one who would stand toe to toe with me as an equal partner. I love your independence, your passion, your sense of fun."

She watched him, trying to absorb the implications of marriage to this man. It would mean such changes, big changes. "I haven't been part of that kind of a team for a long time," she said. "I've grown very independent since then. I do things my own way."

"We'd both have to make adjustments."

"Sometimes that isn't enough," she said. "You have to begin right, wanting the same things." She dropped her gaze to their clasped hands, remembering another beginning that had seemed so promising. The memory was too old to still hurt but clear enough to temper her joy over Matt's proposal. She shivered and reached for the comforter, wrapping it around her to ward off the chill of the air-conditioner now that the heat of passion had cooled. He tucked it around her shoulders, then took her hands in his again.

"I'll be honest with you, Matt," she said. "I'm very tempted, especially now when I'm sitting here in your bed where we just made magnificent love. I want very much to marry you. But I know how it feels to want and then watch it all fall apart."

He leaned over, kissing her lightly on the forehead. "I'm sorry. It's too soon. Forget for now that I asked."

She looked at him in amazement. "I can't forget something like that."

"All right. We'll put it on the back burner for a while. We have a few weeks left before either of us has to move on to another location."

Abby nodded. "It would give us time to get to know one another better."

"Good." He sprawled back on the bed, pulling her with him. Then he rolled, pulling them both over until they were trapped in the warmth of the cover like two campers tied into a single mummy bag.

She laughed as she nestled her head against his shoulder. "Matt, what do you want from life? Where do you want to be five years from now, ten years, twenty?"

He smiled. "Where doesn't matter. Here, in a mountain cabin, on a tropical island. I want somebody to share breakfast with, to laugh at my jokes, even when they're dumb. Somebody who will still love me when my hair and teeth are gone."

She let her eyes sink closed. "That sounds wonderful."

"It could be us," he said. "We could go anywhere, do anything. Think about it."

"I am."

Her eyelids drifted closed. She lay there, imagining a life at Matt's side. Yet the picture wasn't complete. He hadn't mentioned children. Maybe his imagination needed to catch up with hers. She shifted, snuggling closer still as the seductive lassitude of sleep stole closer. She had just drifted off when he whispered her name.

"Hmmm?" She heard the strong, steady rhythm of his heartbeat beneath her ear. Solid and dependable, yet she could make it race with a delicate touch in the right place.

"Tell me about the dolphins. Tell me why they mean so much to you."

He stroked her hair as if he couldn't bear not to touch her. It made her feel cherished and loved. At that moment, she would have done almost anything for him.

"The dolphins?" She forced her thoughts to her work and the reasons it had become so important to her. "I want people to see them and learn to respect them."

"Why dolphins? Why not pet poodles?"

Abby chuckled softly. "My porpoises are much more special than any pet poodle."

"Tell me."

"About eight years ago I went to work for Marine Shows. It was a much smaller operation then, and the director was an old friend of Pop's, somebody he met when he was overseas in the navy.

"I'd been there a few months and had spent some

time assisting in the shows and even in some of the training. Then one day Jonathan put me in with Butterfly. She's the grande dame of Marine Shows, the first porpoise of theirs to give birth in captivity. Otto is one of her calves."

"So you've been with Otto from the beginning."

"Off and on," she said, stifling a yawn.

"Continue, please."

"Well, I was in the water with her and I got my signals mixed up. I told her to leap high instead of wave to the crowd. Her splash half drowned me. She swam close to me, almost like she was treading water, until I caught my breath. She nuzzled me a couple of times, reassuring me, I guess. Then she disappeared. She swam up behind me and poked me in the back, not hard enough to hurt but hard enough to get my attention."

He laughed. "And she's Otto's mother? That explains a few things."

"It does, doesn't it?" she agreed. "Anyway, I was hooked. It sounds weird, but I felt as if I'd made a new friend. She seemed to pick up on my moods, playful sometimes, quiet others. Jonathan explained how they communicate with sonar, and how they can pick up the pulse rate of a human in the water. I found that Butterfly became really excited when I was. When I ignored her or when I was feeling lazy and relaxed, she stayed pretty low key."

"That makes sense."

"After a while," she continued, "I started wearing a face mask to work underwater. You start the training underwater and only move on to the leaps above the surface after the dolphin has mastered the basic movements," she explained.

"Anyway, I was treading water one afternoon, just

taking a breather. Butterfly swam slowly toward me, watching me with her left eye just below the water's surface. I sank down a bit so I could see her better, and she moved closer. It was more than just her watching me. It was as if she was looking *in* me with this powerful eye, like some alien scanner on *Science Fiction Theater*. A mind lock of some sort, I guess. It was an amazing experience. I could feel bubbles of sound, her sonar, I think, all through me and I wished I could understand what she was saying. It was like meeting some very wise, very old woman who could tell me everything I wanted to know, but not in any language I could understand."

Matt remained silent for a moment. "That's fascinating," he finally said. "Has this happened with any of the others?"

"Not like that. Only with Butterfly."

He squeezed her tightly. "Thank you for telling me." He twisted, throwing off the cover. "Come on, it's getting too warm in here."

"For you maybe. I was just getting comfortable."

"Come on. I'll show you comfortable." He walked over to the doors, unself-conscious in his nakedness. His body was firm without being overly muscled. Lean and strong, with long runner's legs. She smiled, thinking she'd guessed the secret of his fitness.

He switched off the lights, throwing the room into darkness. She could hear the low hum of the bubbling jets of the hot tub, seducing her with the promise of a hot water massage.

"The water's warm," he said.

"I'll be right there." She waited until he'd left the room before she sat up. As her eyes adjusted to the darkness, she saw the scattered evidence of their lovemaking, the rumpled bedcovers, the pillows that had fallen to the floor, her black pantyhose dangling from a lamp shade in the corner. She giggled all the way to the bathroom.

A moment later, she slipped through the sliding glass door and glanced at the stars overhead. She felt self-conscious, walking around naked in this glass-walled room.

"It's fine. There's a wall around the entire back garden, and none of the neighbors have any windows facing this side. I already checked," Matt said, sensing her hesitancy. "Besides, it's reflective glass. Nobody can see in during the day, and not at night either unless there's a light on."

Feeling slightly silly, Abby hurried over to the bubbling water and dipped a tentative toe beneath the surface. It felt wonderful, soft and soothing water caresses. She lowered herself into the froth and sighed. "This is heaven." She sat on the smooth shelf opposite Matt, content to laze back and enjoy the sensations.

They sat there in silence for a while, staring at the stars and letting the bubbling jets wash away all thoughts of tomorrow. Or so she thought.

She glanced over to find him watching her, his eyes shadowed in the starlight. "I think I could get used to this," she said.

He reached across, drawing her closer. His kiss was possessive, with a thread of passion humming beneath the tenderness. He lifted his head and stared at her for a long moment.

"What do you really want, Abby? What are you holding back from me?"

Abby's hand stilled. "Holding back?" she repeated.

"You've always kept a part of yourself locked away. You're cautious, but it's more than that. These plans of yours, could they include me?"

She remained silent a moment, wondering what to tell him, how much to risk. If she was pregnant, she had to tell him. She couldn't deceive him into a marriage with one person more than he'd bargained for. On the other hand, if she wasn't, that part of her life could remain untold.

"Some things are very personal," she said. "It's not something I've felt like broadcasting. I guess a part of me has been afraid of frightening you away."

"I don't frighten easily."

She smiled against his bare chest. "I know. It's hard to explain. I hadn't pictured myself marrying a corporate troubleshooter who jets around the country on a regular basis. I guess I always imagined something like what my parents had."

"A house, station wagon, and 2.5 children," he filled in.

"Something like that."

"I guess I had you pegged as a career woman."

"Women today want it all," she reminded him.

"It's not as rosy as it appears," he said. "Have you thought about the mortgage, bills to pay, diapers, midnight feedings, pacing the hallway in the emergency room? I've seen more than one woman crack under the combined pressure. I don't think any of us can have it all. Besides, I hear childbirth itself is pure hell."

Abby chuckled. "I've heard that, too."

"You're from a big family," he said. "I suppose it's natural you'd have these kinds of expectations. But are they your dreams or just what you're expected to do?"

She already knew the answer to that. She'd gone beyond anything her parents had considered reasonable, had shocked her father beyond belief. Matt was a man like her father in that respect. He wouldn't understand this overwhelming need to have a child. And she couldn't have him unless he tried.

"It's hard to explain," she said. "It's so tangled up that I don't know how to put it into words. Believe me, I've tried. Pop thinks I'm nuts."

"Try me," he said.

Abby thought for a moment, searching for the words. "It's all about love, about being part of something bigger than myself. It's odd, but I think that's something else Butterfly taught me."

"Now I'm lost."

"I was in Tulsa right after Otto was born. Late one afternoon, I was dangling my feet in the water and Butterfly bumped me a couple of times. Then she came up and took my hand between her teeth, holding it and tugging it a little. Not enough to hurt, though she could have if she wanted to.

"I figured she was trying to tell me something. I got my mask and jumped in with her and Otto. It was like that other time, the humming, bubbling sensation, and that mesmerizing eye contact. I couldn't look away. I didn't even think of it. I don't know how long it lasted. They swam around for a while, moving together in rhythm. Otto mimicked her every move and then slipped away from her. She bumped him and he got right back into place. Then he nursed. That's when I understood. She looked at me again, and I didn't need to translate the signals of this sonar language because I could feel the mother love."

"I always knew that someday I'd have it for myself, that I had to. I want a child, Matt."

He stiffened. "That's the one thing I can't give you." He sounded empty, completely vacant of emotion.

Abby studied his expression, frightened by his sudden withdrawal. "What do you mean?"

"I can't have children, Abby."

She touched his face lovingly, trying to smooth away the frown. "So what? I don't love you because of your sperm count, for heaven's sake. That's not why I want to be with you. Besides, there are other alternatives."

He captured her hand, drawing it away from his face. He clenched his fists around her smaller ones, holding them in the churning water. "You don't understand, Abby. Listen to me. I don't want children. I had a vasectomy."

She went limp. She stared at him vacantly, trying to absorb what he'd just said. He shook his head helplessly, pulling her against him.

"Why?"

"I decided a long time ago that I didn't want to be a father. So I made sure."

She felt a chill deep within her. She could see everything she'd hoped for crumbling around her while it was still half built. "You're so good with the boys. They think you're terrific."

"I think they're terrific, too. I can be an uncle and a friend. But I can't be a father, Abby. It's something I accepted a long time ago. If I could change things now, I would. But I can't." She saw the deep furrows in his brow, the tense set of his jaw.

"Sometimes, when we're young—" he began, but she stopped him with a quick kiss.

"Please, Matt. We'll figure out something. Don't worry about it. Vasectomies are reversible. I've even heard of nature reversing them on its own. I'll bet that was a surprise, finding out the little tubes had grown back in place."

He shook his head. "No, Abby. You don't understand. I like children, but I don't want the permanent responsibility of a child. I don't want the worries or the sleepless nights wondering whether it's just a cough or something more serious. Please understand. I'd give you anything you want, anything but that. I just can't. I can't be a father. I won't.'' The words seemed to be wrenched out of him in rejection of a role he couldn't bear to accept.

She couldn't think of anything to say. She touched his cheek with the back of her hand, barely registering the faint scratch of whisker stubble through her pain. Through his pain. It cut her to the soul, this stabbing regret about which she could do nothing. She hadn't realized how deeply his sister's illness had hurt him. His parents' loss marked his life so deeply that he made sure he'd never risk losing a child. A man who must deal with huge risks in business life, he couldn't take the biggest personal risk of all.

''Oh, God,'' she murmured. ''I didn't know. I just didn't know.''

He pulled away from her and climbed out of the hot tub. He stood there for a moment, watching her. He ran damp fingers through his hair distractedly before he slowly turned and walked away, leaving Abby alone under the stars.

Two more days passed before Abby worked up the courage to break the seal on the small box holding the second pregnancy test. She laid the contents out in a row on her dresser, then sank onto the bed, staring at them.

Caught between the proverbial rock and a hard place, she couldn't face knowing. No matter what the outcome, she would lose something she treasured. If she was pregnant, she got her deepest wish. But she also faced losing the man she loved.

And if she was not pregnant?

She leaned forward, burying her head in her hands. Her choices weren't so clear-cut anymore. She'd told Pop she'd try again and again until she succeeded. Now she wasn't so sure. Maybe she could simply accept the failure as a sign that it was not meant to be.

She looked at the kit again. The requisite ten days had elapsed yesterday. She could take the test and know now or wait for a definitive sign from Mother Nature, a sign due soon anyway. She picked up the little cup that came with the kit and headed for the bathroom. She couldn't stand not knowing.

Moments later, she hovered over the dresser, waiting to see whether the little circle would form in the test tube. A soft knock at the door drew her attention but only for an instant. "Yes," she answered absently.

The door swung open. "Oh," Bethany said, her eyes focusing on the test kit. She stepped inside and gently closed the door behind her. "Well?"

"I don't know yet," Abby answered, glancing at her sister. "I just started the test."

"Why didn't you get one of those quick kits, those stick ones?" Bethany asked.

"The store was out of them."

Bethany nodded anxiously, then crooked her finger. "Come sit with me." She sank onto the old quilt that served as Abby's bedspread, then patted the spot beside her. "Talk to me a minute."

"I can't."

"It's like watching water and waiting for it to boil. It'll never happen with you hanging over it, breathing on it."

Abby tried to smile. The stiff twist of her lips was an utter failure. "I know what you're trying to do, but I'm too nervous."

"And you're making me nervous."

Abby glanced at her watch, then peered down the tube. She saw nothing but a few murky droplets, the same as fifteen seconds ago. "You're right." She flopped onto the bed beside her sister and groaned.

"Jeez, I can't believe you're doing this," Bethany muttered. She laid back, staring at the ceiling. "Remember when we were kids. We said we'd never grow up to be like our parents. Now here you are, contemplating motherhood."

Abby grinned down at Bethany. "We aren't like them. Think about it. You're still marching for toxic waste cleanup and saving the wolves. And I'm getting pregnant by remote control, as Pop puts it."

Bethany snorted. "He has such a way with words."

"I've noticed. He's come up with all sorts of colorful descriptions for what I'm doing."

"Ignore him. He's doing the best he can."

"Actually, sis, he's been much better than I expected. Yesterday he offered to be my birthing partner. I think he's been reading my books."

"Oh, no." Bethany covered her face with her hands in mock despair. "Spare us from Pop and the books. He'll be quoting reproductive trivia at the dinner table."

"It won't bother me. I won't be there," Abby retorted. "If I'm pregnant, I probably will be spending the next few months hanging over the toilet. Morning sickness runs in the family, according to Pop and Maureen."

Bethany groaned again. "I think I'll stick to the toxic waste and wolves. At least they don't play havoc with my appetite."

Abby looked at her watch again. "Almost time."

Bethany grabbed her arm. "Don't you dare. Not

yet.'' She sat up, her expression anxious. ''Have you told Matt about this yet?''

Abby shook her head slowly. ''I don't know what to do. He asked me to marry him.''

''Do you love him?''

Abby nodded. ''So much it hurts. But he doesn't want children. I don't think he's going to change his mind.''

Bethany looked startled. ''You're kidding! Matt Gardner doesn't like kids. He could have fooled me.''

Abby jumped to her feet and paced the bare wood floor. ''It's not that he doesn't like them. I think he's afraid. His sister died, and he has some pretty deep scars from the experience. Bethany, he had a vasectomy.''

Her sister looked stricken. ''My God, Abby.''

''That's how I feel.'' She glanced over at the test tube, then back at her sister. ''You look. I can't.'' She sank onto the bed, her hands clenched into fists.

Bethany walked slowly to the dresser and peered down into the test tube. Then she straightened and turned to Abby, her expression frozen. ''There's a ring in the bottom.''

''I'm pregnant,'' Abby said. She touched her flat abdomen. ''I'm pregnant,'' she repeated, feeling numb. A week ago, the news would have brought wild shrieks of joy. But that was when she still thought she could have it all. Now she knew she couldn't.

''Do you want me to tell Pop?''

Abby shook her head. ''I'll do it. And don't mention anything else I told you, either. Pop doesn't need to know the rest.''

''And Matt?'' Bethany wore a helpless expression as she laid a comforting hand on Abby's shoulder.

''There's nothing you can do. I still have to figure that one out,'' Abby replied.

Bethany hugged her, long and hard. "It'll work out," she whispered huskily. "I know it will. He's crazy about you. He'll understand."

"Maybe you're right," Abby said. She didn't believe it, though. Bethany hadn't seen the look on his face or heard the pain in his voice. Matt's scars went too deep.

TEN

Three days later, a blood test at the clinic confirmed Abby's pregnancy. So Abby finally told her father. His response was predictably gruff, though she caught him several times after that with his nose immersed in one of her childbirth books. And all sources of caffeine and junk food disappeared from the house, replaced by low-fat milk, fruit, and raw vegetables.

But she didn't tell Matt about the baby. Even if she had wanted to, she couldn't. He'd gone back to New York for a special board meeting concerning the expansion project. One day passed into the next that week with no more than a brief phone call between his meetings. By Friday, missing him had become a physical ache, even though she knew that his return would only bring the moment of confession nearer.

The telephone was ringing in the pit when she came through the door after her midafternoon show. She picked it up, speaking in a desultory tone.

"Bad day?" The sound of Matt's voice lifted her spirits immediately, unknotting the ball of tension that had grown since Otto tried to jump over the edge of the pool early this morning.

"It hasn't been great," Abby said.

"Is Otto giving you trouble again, love?" His tone was warm and intimate, as if they'd never disagreed on such a vital point as whether or not to have children. It was as if the week of silence had never happened.

"Otto's a brat, but it's nothing I can't handle," she replied edgily. She didn't want to talk about Otto. But she didn't want to tell him about the baby either, not now and not like this.

The silence on the line stretched between them. She leaned back against the wall, squeezing her eyes closed and trying to think of a way to begin. This wasn't something that could be settled long-distance. And it wasn't something that had to be settled today.

"So how's business?" she finally asked. "Are we getting the seal pool?"

Matt laughed. "Is that all you think about? What about me?"

Abby winced, her hand silently lowering to touch her flat abdomen. "I think about a lot of things," she murmured, her throat tight again.

"Sorry, I shouldn't tease," he said, his tone more serious. "Abby, we really need to talk. Not like this, but face to face."

"I agree."

"I'm taking an early flight tomorrow," he said. "I'll come over to the dolphin pool when I get in."

"All right," she agreed.

"And Abby? We'll figure out something. I think when I explain why, you'll understand that we simply can't have children." She could feel the emotion vibrating in his voice, even through the artificial distortions of distance and electronic instruments.

"I can't talk about this now, Matt," she said, barely breathing. "I need to see you before I—" She clenched her eyes closed, unable to finish. She needed to touch him, to kiss him and have him love her again before she gave him up.

"Before you what?" he asked, sounding suddenly uneasy.

"Nothing, Matt. I just need to see you. We'll talk tomorrow." She hung up the phone before he could answer. Then she turned and went out the back door, locking it behind her. She didn't want to be alone with her thoughts. She needed to be with people, to talk and laugh and forget about the tangled mess her life had become.

So she grabbed Bethany, and the two sisters spent the next hour playing hooky in the park, riding the roller coasters, sipping snow cones, and pretending that Abby's problem didn't exist. And when Abby's shift ended late that night, Bethany was waiting in the parking lot on the hood of Abby's car.

"I thought you rode with the carpool today?"

Bethany grimaced as she slid down off the hood. "I did. But I had a few things to finish up before Matt comes back. I figured it was better to stay late tonight than to come in over the weekend."

Abby aimed a playful jab in her direction. "Spoken like a true white-collar employee. Tell me, how does it feel to look out of your air-conditioned office at the rest of us poor slobs sweltering in the heat?"

Bethany waited until Abby unlocked her door, then turned a Cheshire smile on her sister. "It's sweet. Very sweet."

"Witch," Abby retorted. She climbed in and started the car.

"Heard any good gossip lately?" Bethany asked,

then proceeded to fill Abby in on the various tales about one of the dancers in the Wild West show.

Abby was still laughing when they pulled into the driveway. "You have to feel sorry for the poor girl," she said. "It must have been horrible, being stranded on the Skylift like that, with nothing but her tights and a naked cowboy to protect her."

"That'll teach her to not take her clothes off in a high wind," Bethany retorted. "It's a good thing it was after hours." Her laughter trailed off when the headlights beamed on the low-slung red MG parked in the narrow driveway.

"He said he was coming back tomorrow," Abby muttered, backing out and parking along the front sidewalk instead.

"Either Matt changed his mind or Pop's taste in cars has changed." Her sarcasm fell on silence as they watched Matt climb out of the driver's seat. He walked around the car and stood, facing them, his expression unreadable.

"You go on in," Abby said.

She waited until Bethany was inside, then slowly opened her door. She got out, then hesitated a moment, gathering her courage. Finally, she made her way across the asphalt, one step at a time, to where he stood. It was probably the most difficult twenty feet she'd ever walked.

"I didn't want to wake your father, so I just waited out here," Matt said when she stopped a few feet from him.

"You said you were coming back tomorrow." To her relief, she sounded much calmer than she felt. Maybe this wouldn't be as difficult as she'd imagined.

"I caught an earlier flight. I couldn't wait. I wouldn't have slept anyway. I had this horrible feeling that you wouldn't be here when I got back." He closed the distance between them, wrapping his arms around her.

She clutched him close. "I'm here. I'm not going anywhere just yet."

She felt him stiffen against her, though he didn't let her go. "Just yet? Then you are planning to leave." He sounded shocked and coldly angry.

"I didn't say that."

"It's about what happened Saturday night, isn't it? I rushed you, took advantage of the situation."

Abby shook her head, pulling away. "Come on, let's talk," she said. She led him to the pair of webbed chairs on the porch.

"Matt," she began when they both were settled. "I told you I have plans for my life. That plan includes children. I'm not twenty-three anymore."

"And you're not sixty either," he said.

She was silent for a moment, then tried again. "Earlier this year, I had a large cyst removed from my right ovary. It was nothing serious, just a little warning that plenty can go wrong with the female reproductive system. I want to have my children before something really does go wrong."

His chair squeaked as he leaned forward, letting his hands dangle between his knees. "So this is the biological clock ticking away."

She glanced helplessly over at him. "Tick, tock," she whispered.

He ran his fingers through his wavy hair. "And you thought I was the father you'd been waiting for."

Abby jumped to her feet, stung by his bitter tone. "Damn it, Matt Gardner, that is a hell of a conclusion to jump to. That is *not* what I thought. You pursued me, not the other way around. I didn't ask to fall in love with you and I didn't trick you into sleeping with me." She paced angrily, then stopped in front of him. He straightened, eyeing her speculatively. Then he rose to his feet with deliberate slowness.

"But in the end, you did make yourself available," he said coolly. "Very available. Did you decide that I fit the medical profile? Or was it the financially secure requirement?"

Abby slapped him hard. Her palm tingled with pin-points of pain, but it was nothing next to the twisting knife in her heart. Matt didn't move, didn't break his unwavering stare as the red imprint of her hand colored his cheek, standing out against his pale skin like a wine stain on white linen. His eyes were cold, calculating which point might be most vulnerable, she decided. She didn't like this side of him, not at all. But she could see now where he'd earned his reputation.

"You can leave now," she said.

His lips twisted into a caricature of the smile she'd fallen in love with. "But what kind of a gentleman would I be if I didn't see my *lady* safely inside?"

"I think I know the answer to that," she said, leaning back against the porch rail.

"Spell it out."

"All right," she began angrily. "A gentleman wouldn't treat the woman he claimed to love this way. You're the user, Matt. Not me. I think you simply wanted to string me along for however many weeks you stick around. And you found out exactly what buttons to push to get your way. You're exactly what I thought you were, right from the beginning. Only I just didn't guess how low you'd stoop."

He reached out for her, but she flung his hand away. "Don't touch me. You make me feel dirty," she retorted, wiping at the tears that were beginning to spill over.

By the time she finished, the last of the color had drained from his face. "No, Abby."

"I don't understand people like you," she whispered, looking away.

He took a step toward her, touching her cheek tentatively. "I'm sorry, Abby. I didn't mean it. I thought . . . I don't know what I thought. You make me crazy. I guess that means I love you."

Abby held her breath, wanting to believe him so badly. Damn, she was too susceptible to his charm. She was too damn needy. She had to get away from him and think. But already she could feel herself relenting, sliding back into the web of his charm. In a swift, smooth movement that was more childhood memory than conscious thought, she slipped over the rail, leaping beyond the shrubbery. She hit the ground running. She crashed through the hedge and sprinted through the neighbor's yard, then cut across a side street toward the old cemetery. She kept running until she reached the sagging iron gates, then let herself inside. She slowed some as she dodged between the shadowy headstones toward the familiar corner against the stone wall. And then she sank onto the ground beneath the arching branches of an overgrown mock-orange bush.

Abby didn't know how long she cried or when she fell asleep. She awoke as the orange glow of dawn warmed the eastern skyline. Cold and stiff from the night on the ground, she pushed her way to her feet and groaned. Mom used to say that everything looked clearer in the morning. Well, it might be clearer, but it wasn't any better.

Abby stretched, trying to ease some of the stiffness from her body. Then she turned toward home, knowing what she had to do. A transfer was the only answer.

She knew herself too well. If Matt wanted, he could persuade her that everything would work out, and for a while, she might even believe him.

But Abby was pregnant. And Matt had adamantly refused to be a father in any sense of the word, even before she'd considered asking him. So she had to choose between the man she loved and the child she craved. She couldn't have both.

She knew there were other options, that she could be rid of the child more easily than she'd gotten it. But that wasn't an alternative, at least not one she'd consider. She pushed the ugly idea away without a second thought. She'd willfully given this child life, and now she had a responsibility to give him or her the best future possible.

She turned her face toward the sunrise, smiling at the golden streaks painting warmth across the sky. Soon, too soon, the sun would burn the chill from the air. But now, it was simply beautiful, the promise of a new beginning for a new day.

So she'd made a mistake. She'd probably make a lot more. But she'd be all right. One step at a time, one foot in front of the other, she'd make it. She had to. Now there was someone special depending on her.

Matt's car was gone when she arrived home, but that's what she'd expected anyway. She tiptoed into the house and up the stairs. Bethany must have been listening for her, though.

"Abby, is that you?"

Abby kicked off her shoes and pushed open her sister's door. "I'm sorry. I didn't mean to wake you."

Bethany yawned, then kicked off the covers. "It's all right. I've been worried. I heard you and Matt fighting."

Abby frowned. "Did Pop hear?"

"I don't think so. You went to the cemetery, didn't you?"

A sheepish smile crossed Abby's lips. "It's the place to go for good advice," she said. "Some of my best friends are there: Tommy, Mom."

"I think it's morbid."

"Maybe, but that cemetery is the only peaceful place around here," Abby retorted.

Bethany didn't look convinced, but then she never seemed to feel the need to escape. "Whatever," she muttered. "Come on. I want to show you something."

"What?"

"Just come with me," her sister said, her face set in that exasperated look that Abby knew better than to argue with.

She followed her sister down the hall to her own room, then froze, her heart caught in her throat. Matt was stretched out on her bed with one of Abby's fat, fluffy pillows clutched to his chest in a sleeping embrace.

"What's he doing here?" Abby demanded angrily, her voice a high, hissing whisper.

"His car is in the garage," Bethany said. "I knew you wouldn't come home as long as you thought he was here. And I also think you're an idiot for running away from him instead of talking about your problems."

"You didn't hear the things he said."

Bethany winced. "Yes, I did. I was listening at the window."

Abby shot her an outraged look.

"Well, what did you think I'd do?" She turned around and stepped into the hall. "Now talk to the man." The door clicked closed.

Abby stared at the porcelain knob for a moment, then swiveled her gaze to the man on the bed. In sleep, he looked vulnerable. The harsh lines were nothing more than faint thread marks across his forehead. She touched his cheek, loving the warm, bristly feel of the unshaven morning shadow. It felt real and alive as it rasped against her soft palm.

"You're back," he whispered as his eyelids fluttered open. "Your sister said you'd be all right, but I didn't believe her. She said you probably would stay with a friend."

Abby smiled sadly. "She was right." Her quiet lost friends couldn't help her now. She had to handle this herself.

"I was worried." Matt caught her hands, crushing them in his relief. "I'm sorry for the things I said. I know you're not like that."

She bit her lip, looking away so he wouldn't see the tears that prickled, threatening to flow freely. "I'm sorry, too. I should never have let it go this far."

He caught her hand, stroking lightly with his thumb. "I didn't understand how strongly you feel about children. And I didn't understand how much I love you. I wish I could be everything you want me to be."

She looked into his eyes, letting him see her tears. "I'm not asking you to change."

He gathered her close to him. "I love you so much, more than I ever could have believed possible."

"Sometimes love isn't enough," she said.

"And sometimes it is," he countered.

She pulled back, smiling. "I think that there's an optimist buried beneath that cool, businesslike brain of yours."

"There's a desperate man on his knees praying," he answered.

"For what?"

"A second chance."

Abby sobered, then leaned toward him, kissing him

briefly on the lips. "Let's slow down and not take ourselves so seriously," she said. "We don't have to solve everything today. We can just enjoy ourselves for the next few weeks and see what happens. If it's meant to be, it will be." She felt as if she was granting herself a reprieve. It wasn't right, but she couldn't let him go. Not yet.

His arms circled around her waist, pulling her back against him. "Sound advice from a wise woman," he whispered, nuzzling her closer.

They drifted to sleep that way and didn't awaken until hours later when the house was silent and empty. Matt, already late for a meeting, hurried home to change while Abby quickly threw on a swimsuit and a pair of shorts and headed for the park.

The next few weeks followed the same pattern as before their night together, quiet picnics and stolen kisses in hidden corners. Plus, there were candlelight dinners at Matt's apartment, boisterous Saturday mornings with Abby's nephews, and peaceful hours under the stars with the long telescope. But Matt didn't mention marriage again, and Abby didn't mention babies. It was an unspoken agreement that kept the peace.

Days passed into weeks, and weeks into months until the hot humid days of summer faded in a cool snap in early September. The crowds at the park were smaller now and were limited to weekends. The rest of the time was reserved for school groups, company picnics, and the seasonal maintenance work that couldn't be done when the park was open daily.

Abby and Jay were entangled in one such project when the bulldog-faced architect arrived at the dolphin arena one crisp afternoon.

"What are you two doing?"

Abby glanced up from the section of speaker wire

she was trying to unsnarl. "Practicing our knots. We're getting pretty good."

The man shook his head and walked past them toward the bottom row of bleachers. "Got something here I want you to look at. These are the final plans for the new aquacenter."

Abby looked at Jay. "Aquacenter?" they said in unison. Abby laughed and tossed down the wire.

"That's what they're calling it," the architect responded. "I just draw 'em. I don't name 'em. What are you two doing anyway?"

Jay grinned. "It's an experiment. There's a group of kids coming in from the children's rehab ward this weekend. We thought maybe we'd hook up a couple of microphones closer to the pool so the kids could hear Otto and Pepper better, maybe even hear them breathe if we can get the equipment set up right."

"Maybe you'd better hire a professional," he said, shaking his head. "Look, I'm running a bit late. Why don't you two check these over and jot down any comments? Then leave them with your friend, Mr. Gardner."

"No problem," Jay answered, bending over the plans.

Half an hour later, Abby stood outside Matt's office, the plans in one hand and two cans of soda in the other. The minute he hung up the phone, she breezed in and dropped the plans on his desk.

"Well?" he asked.

She handed him a soda and grinned. "Just about perfect."

"Good. I ordered a pizza," he said, checking his watch. "It should be here any time."

"Anchovies?" she asked.

"Only on my half, though I can't imagine why you object to cooked fish on your pizza when you put those raw herring tails in your mouth several times a day."

"That's different. It's just part of the job. An unpleasant part, I'll admit."

He still looked unconvinced as he stared down at the inevitable computer printout on his desk. "Whatever you say."

Abby smiled. "I say that I have tonight off and I'd like to spend it with you," she said with an abrupt change of the subject. "We don't have much time left."

Matt glanced up from the printout. "The offer still stands," he reminded her.

She looked away. "We can talk about that later. Right now, I think I smell a pizza boy." She jumped up from the chair and leaned out the door.

"Well?"

Abby glanced over her shoulder. "He's down the hall at accounting right now. Looks like they ordered two pizzas."

A moment later, the delivery boy stepped through Matt's doorway and set the pizza on the credenza where Matt indicated. Matt paid him, while Abby raided Bethany's stash of napkins in the file cabinet of the publicity office. When she walked back into Matt's office, he was perched on the credenza, already munching on a piece.

The warm, spicy pizza smell hit her full force as she stepped through the doorway. But instead of sparking growls of hunger, a wave of nausea caught in her throat.

"It's good," Matt said between bites, completely oblivious to her discomfort.

"I'll bet." Abby picked up a slice from her half and took a bite. A second wave of nausea welled up, stronger than the first. Abby dropped the slice and headed down the hallway at a half run.

Bethany found her in the women's restroom ten minutes later, slumped over the sink. She splashed another handful of cool water on her face and stood up. Her eyes were red-rimmed from crying, and she was too pale.

"Abby, what happened?" her sister asked, bending over her.

Abby shook her head. "The term 'morning sickness' is a lie. Does it look like morning out there to you?" She sniffed hard, then wiped the back of her hand across her eyes, smearing what remained of her mascara.

Bethany pulled a paper towel from the dispenser and handed it to Abby, who dabbed around her eyes at the black smears. "Matt's really worried. He thinks you may be coming down with that virus that's been going around."

Abby nodded. "He sent you in here, didn't he?"

"You haven't told him you're pregnant yet," Bethany surmised.

Abby glanced up, a fresh set of tears welling forth. "I can't get the words out. I'm not ready to give him up."

"You don't know that you'll have to."

Abby clenched her eyes closed. "For some reason, he can't bear to be responsible for a child."

"A lot of thirty-eight-year-old bachelors feel that way," Bethany retorted.

"This isn't your run-of-the-mill bachelor thing. Bethany, he can't even talk about it. I know it has something to do with his sister dying so young and being disabled and all. He has this horrible fear. I could see it in his face."

"Pretty soon you'll start to show," Bethany reminded her.

"I know," Abby said, starting for the door.

"Abby? I'll tell him if you want me to."

Abby shook her head. "Thanks, but no thanks. I have to do this myself." She pushed open the door and stepped out. Now she knew how those prisoners from the pirate stories felt when they walked the plank.

Matt leaned against the opposite wall, looking exactly as she'd expected, slightly anxious, yet ready to tease her out of any uncomfortable feelings she might have about running out that way.

"The anchovies apologize and promise never to jump onto your side of the pizza again," he said. He pushed away from the wall and took her hand.

Abby had to smile. "If you don't mind, I think I'll keep my distance from the pizza for a while."

"I'll take you home." It wasn't an offer but a statement of fact.

She shook her head. "I'll be all right."

"Not a chance," he said, taking her hand and leading her back to the office. "Your sister can tell Jay and somebody can bring your car later."

Abby started to argue, but a waft of pizza odor nearly sent her back to the restroom. She quelled the urge and swallowed hard. "Maybe I would feel better if I lay down for a while."

Matt draped his suit jacket over her shoulders and snapped off the light switch. "Wait by the door and I'll go get the car."

Abby leaned back against the wall and nodded, feeling too nauseated to argue with him at the moment. She remained silent on the short drive home, wondering whether she should go ahead and tell him or wait until she felt better. If she ever felt better.

Pop wasn't at home, so Matt insisted on seeing her safely to her room and tucking her under a warm afghan. "I'll call later," he said, bending low to kiss her forehead. Abby nodded slowly, fighting off another wave of nausea. Maybe this was more than morning sickness. It sure felt awful enough to be the flu. But just in case, she'd dig into the soda crackers the minute Matt left.

He hesitated at the door, his eyes scanning the room, then coming back to rest on her. "Are you sure there's nothing else you need?"

"I'll be all right," she assured him, then froze as his gaze shifted to the dresser top next to him. He picked up the stack of books, all on birthing and pregnancy except the top one.

"*You and Your Baby*," he read aloud, looking disturbed.

"Matt, I—"

He held up a hand, stopping her. "You don't have to explain. You told me how you felt. I'd just hoped you would change your mind."

"I haven't," she said, her voice barely above a whisper.

He nodded sadly. "That's what I was afraid of." He set the books on the dresser and left. Every slow, heavy step down the hall and on the stairs felt like a hammer blow to Abby's heart. The faraway click of the front door seemed like the final beat before her heart stopped.

Before she had time to dwell on it, though, the phone rang next to her bed. She picked up the receiver, speaking in a desultory tone.

"Soda crackers and lemon wedges," her older sister said.

"Maureen?"

"Bethany called and said that the nausea bug finally hit," Maureen said. "The secret is to not let your stomach get empty. Eat small meals and more often. And keep munching on those crackers. When the nausea gets really bad, suck on a lemon wedge. That works for seasickness, too.''

Abby laughed weakly. ''I'll remember that.''

The minute Maureen hung up, Abby bounded out of bed and headed for the kitchen. She found an unopened box of crackers in the cabinet, then sliced a lemon and stuck a wedge between her teeth.

''Ugh!'' she grumbled, puckering with the tartness. She carried it and the crackers upstairs, all the while wondering whether it would do any good.

Back in her bed, she picked up her address book and dialed a number she'd hoped she wouldn't have to use. ''Uncle Robert,'' she said when the director picked up his private line. ''I need a favor.''

Three days later, she'd figured out the pattern of her nausea and regained a semblance of control over her life. Plastic storage bags of saltines and lemon wedges accompanied her to work, along with her supply of light snack food to get her through the early part of the day. By three o'clock on most days, the nausea vanished, only to return late in the evening. She stuck with her sister's advice and avoided heavy meals. Pizza was something else she stayed away from, simply because the smell evoked memories she'd rather leave buried.

''Feeling better?'' Matt asked one balmy afternoon as he slipped up behind Abby while she worked with Otto at the edge of the pool.

Startled, Abby jerked, then grinned over her shoulder. ''I wish you'd stop doing that. Whistle or something.''

''I keep hoping you'll fall in the pool.''

Abby shrugged. ''That wouldn't be so bad today.''

''Indian summer,'' Matt confirmed. ''I guess this is

it. How soon before the leaves start turning colors out here?"

Abby sobered. "A few weeks yet." She wouldn't be around to see them, though. Uncle Robert had come through with the favor, and all the arrangements had been made for an early transfer to Tulsa. Unless she changed her mind, she'd be gone by the end of the week.

"Something wrong? You're not still feeling under the weather, are you?" he asked. "Maybe you came back to work too soon."

Abby shook her head. "No. I just hate to see the summer end. I'm not much of a winter person." She didn't tell him that her sadness had less to do with the weather and more with leaving. But she had to go. A clean break would be less painful in the long run than the slow withering that would occur if she stayed.

"Dinner tonight?" she asked.

"At Mario's?"

She shook her head. "Only if Mario's has takeout." She wanted privacy tonight. She wanted one last time in his arms before she said good-bye, one last memory to carry her through the long months of pregnancy, and the long years after that.

"I'll pick it up," Matt offered with a warm smile. "Six o'clock?"

"Seven," Abby suggested. "I have to pick up a few things at the store, so it'll take me a while to get there."

"I'll see you at seven, then," Matt said, bending low. His kiss was warm and sensual, filling her with bittersweet longing. For the thousandth time that week, she wished things could have been different for them.

A few hours later, he met her at the door with a single red rose, its color soft and glowing with the natural luster of beeswax. Another flower that could be shaped and reshaped. Surprised, Abby searched his expression for a clue to the reason behind the gesture. But she found only loving warmth, with that faint underlying tension that had been present for weeks now. A tension she shared.

"It's an anniversary present," he informed her.

"Excuse me?"

"We met exactly four months ago today." He turned and hurried back toward the kitchen to shut off a loud buzzing noise. "That's the timer, not the fire alarm," he called.

"For dinner? I thought you were picking something up?"

"I did. It just needed to be warmed."

Abby followed him more slowly, setting the bottle of sparkling grape juice she carried on the counter. Matt smiled when he saw it, then waggled his eyebrows in an exaggerated leer. "You brought bubbly. I guess this means your intentions are dishonorable."

She turned the label so he could see it.

"Oh."

"You seem disappointed."

He pulled a covered dish out of the oven and set it on the counter. "I am," he finally said. "I was hoping you wanted to have your way with me."

Abby chuckled. "I do. And this way, I'll remember every second of it."

Matt glanced over his shoulder. "We could skip dinner."

She stepped closer and ran a finger along his spine in a teasing caress. "We could."

He dropped the lid with a clatter and spun around,

hauling her into his arms with a mock growl. Abby giggled and clutched at his shoulders as he carried her through the house, past the bed, and through the opened double doors to the hot tub.

"It isn't dark yet," Abby reminded him. "What will the neighbors think?"

"I told you before. The neighbors can't see."

"And if they could?" Abby reached for the top button of his polo shirt, popping it nimbly through the buttonhole.

"They'd be jealous," he murmured hoarsely. He pulled her close, kissing her with sweet reverence. And Abby poured her heart into it, allowing her body to tell him how much he meant to her.

They undressed slowly, almost worshipfully. He kissed her again. First her lips, then the sensitive trail down her neck to her breasts, then lower still until Abby thought she would go insane with desire. And still he kissed her, teasing her with mindless pleasure.

"Couldn't we skip the hot tub?" she whispered.

"I think we'd better." He lifted her up and carried her to the wide, soft bed.

"I love you," she whispered, just before he entered her. And then, she was completely incapable of coherent thought, only feelings. Sweet, sensuous, soaring feelings that carried her higher than she'd ever been before.

He whispered her name, over and over, then finally he shuddered with an ecstasy that matched her own. And he called her name once more before he rolled over to lie beside her, folding her into his arms.

Abby lay there quietly, listening to the sound of his heartbeat beneath her ear. Strong and steady, it gave a rhythm to the silence, a rhythm that blended with her every breath. They lay that way for a long time, so silent and still they might have been asleep.

But Abby wasn't. She couldn't waste the time in something so mundane as sleep. Instead, she memorized the feel of him, the texture of the curling chest hairs against her cheek, of his skin where it touched her hip. And she loved him, silently and still hoping that something would happen to make this transfer unnecessary.

His hand lifted from her shoulder to stroke her hair, and he kissed her forehead. Abby kept her eyes closed, savoring the feel of his lips against her skin.

"Oh, Abby," he murmured softly. "Why can't this be enough for you? Why do you need the one thing that's so impossible for me to give you?"

And Abby didn't answer. Even if she'd wanted to, she couldn't have spoken past the lump in her throat. Nothing was going to happen to change her course. Matt wanted her. But he didn't want her child. In time, he might accept the child for Abby's sake. But it wouldn't be the same. And it wouldn't be enough for either of them.

So she just lay there, pretending to be asleep. Hours later, she still lay there, awake and still fitted against Matt's relaxed body. Her silent tears spent, she simply waited, feeling dead inside. She waited for the moment when he was too deeply asleep to wake when she left and waited for the courage to leave.

And finally, she knew she could wait no more. She slid out of his embrace, pausing when he shifted and reached for her. She moved a pillow, fitting it into the circle of his arms, and left his bed.

She dressed hurriedly, gathering up her things from the sunroom, where she'd left them scattered over the floor. Then she stepped into the den and pulled a sheet of paper and a pen from the desk. It took only a moment to write the note because there was very little left to say. It had been a wonderful summer. But now, the summer was over.

She let herself out the front door, then climbed into her already packed car and turned it south toward Tulsa.

ELEVEN

Dear Matt, This is the hardest thing I've ever had to do, but I have to go. We're good together now, but it wouldn't stay that way. It's better to make a clean break of it while the memories are sweet.

Even now, he could remember every word of that note, every bold curl of the pen's stroke. She was wrong, though. It wasn't a clean break, not for him.

Matt stood alone in the office, looking out the broad plate-glass window at the leaping dolphins in the indoor amphitheater below him. The mid-January crowd only half filled the seats, making it easier for him to scan the faces. It had become a habit to look for her whenever his work brought him to a facility contracting with Marine Shows. After three and a half months, he'd stopped expecting to see her, but he couldn't stop himself from looking.

''Mr. Gardner?'' He started, then turned around as he realized that he hadn't even heard the door open.

''Sorry, didn't mean to startle you,'' the bearded man

said in his slightly English accent. He'd run the Florida-based company for more than ten years, but his speech hadn't taken on a hint of the drawl characteristic of this area of the South. Obviously, the man was as obstinate in his personal habits as he was in his negotiations over the terms of the new contract between AmericaLand and Marine Shows.

"I have wondered why AmericaLand sent someone such as yourself to handle a contract that's no more than a formality," he said.

"Normally they wouldn't have," Matt said with a slight shrug. "But your initial offering was somewhat different from our previous contracts. I believe that was due to some trouble at the Kansas City facility. I wanted to personally assure you that the situation has been rectified. Our new man there understands our priorities."

"I do hope so. Aside from the monetary investment, these creatures are . . ." he hesitated, as if searching for the right word. "They're quite special, surprisingly intelligent. I sometimes wonder whether we have any right to treat them like parlor pets. But we all have to make difficult choices in business, isn't that so?"

Matt nodded. "Business is business," he mouthed, almost by rote as he stood and shook the man's hand. A brief smile stole onto his face. "I'll have to confess, too, that this trip isn't strictly business. After I finish here, I'll visit my parents."

"They live in Panama City Beach?"

"East of here. They retired to a little house about a block from the beach."

The director nodded. "It's nice when you can manage to combine these trips. If there's anything else I can help you with, a tour perhaps? We have a new seawater filtration system you might find interesting."

"Another time," Matt answered. "I'd like to fax a copy of the contract to my superior as soon as possible."

"We could do that for you, if you like."

Matt nodded. "I would appreciate that." It took only a moment to make the arrangements, then wait for confirmation that the fax was received in the home office. After that, there was little reason to stay. When he opened the office door, though, the mingled odors of salt water and disinfectant took him back for an instant. He felt a pang of regret for the free-spirited moments with Abby at the pit in the Kansas City park.

He hesitated, then faced the director. "I was wondering, one of your employees, Abby Monroe, was with us in Kansas City during the trouble last summer. She helped us a great deal, even recommended an excellent firm to design the new aquacenter we're building there. I wanted to let her know how things turned out, but we've lost track of her."

"And you'd like me to put you in touch with her?" the director filled in. "I believe I recall the name, but I'm not sure where she is now. We just sent a couple of trainers to Australia for a contract there, but I don't believe that's where she is now. Maybe Barbados," he muttered thoughtfully as he pushed back from his desk and started for the door.

Matt's spirits sank. No wonder he'd been unable to find her. She could be half a world away. "She went to Tulsa and finished the season there, but evidently your company sent her elsewhere for the winter." He'd tried to respect her decision. But she must have known that he was quietly keeping tabs on her, because she'd completely disappeared in November, about the same time that Jay left the park, bound for parts unknown.

The director nodded. "So it seems. Excuse me a

moment and I'll see if I can find a list of the current postings.''

Matt held his breath, struggling to maintain his carefully composed expression as the man hovered in the doorway, speaking softly to his secretary. A moment later he returned, carrying a computer printout. He walked slowly, scanning the pages.

''That's odd,'' he said, sinking heavily into his chair, his face crinkling into a frown above the beard.

''Is there a problem?'' Matt asked, more sharply than he intended.

The director's shrewd gaze flickered over Matt, then back to the page. ''You understand, of course, that even if I had the information you seek, I could not give it to you. I would be willing to convey a message, if that were possible.''

''What do you mean?''

''Ms. Monroe is no longer with this company. And she left no forwarding address.''

Matt waited for the disappointment, the pain of this last failure to register. But he felt nothing, only blessed numbness. ''I see.''

She really did not want to be found. She'd said everything she needed to say in the note she left him. Now he simply had to accept it. Or did he?

''No forwarding address? What happens at tax time when she needs her W-2?''

The director remained impassive. ''I'm sorry, but I can't help you.''

Matt's lips tightened. He nodded slowly and left the room without another word. The numbness lasted until he reached the main entrance. Across the wide lobby, the double doors to the amphitheater swung open. The show was just letting out, and the milling crowd blocked the exit.

His steps slowed, then stopped altogether. It wasn't so much the people blocking his way. It was the humid air, the salty mix of scents drifting out into the corridor, filling his senses more strongly than they had up in the office. Sharp regret stabbed at him, almost choking him. He needed to get out of this place before the smells resurrected a score of memories. He swallowed, trying to dislodge the painful lump in his throat.

"Say good-bye, Matt," he whispered wryly. He'd given Abby too little, too late. Now he had to accept that he'd lost and let her go with good grace. It was an unsatisfactory ending, though, with loose ends and questions left hanging. But it seemed that he was the only one who felt that way.

He started through the crowd toward the exit. That's when he saw Jay, strolling across the far end of the corridor, carrying a jumble of floats, balls, and netting. Matt's chin snapped up. He changed directions, knifing through the crowd with barely a glance for the people he brushed against. But the cross section of hallway was empty when he reached the corner.

He hesitated, looking up the hallway and down, then stepped over the chain guard, ignoring the "employees only" sign. He turned right, following the hallway until he reached a set of double doors leading outside. Beyond them were two painted brick warehouses.

Matt followed an employee bearing buckets of small half-frozen fish into the building on the left. Inside, it looked like a cross between an Olympic training center and a fish farm. Two separate pools occupied most of the space. Wire bins of circus-colored balls and hoops lined the narrow walkway between the pools. At the far corner, a rubber-necked seal balanced a bucket on the tip of its nose. Closer, a group of trainers worked over a canvas sling holding a dolphin that had beached itself.

"Can I help you?" Matt spun on his heel to face a tall, dark-tanned woman with weathered skin and steel-gray hair bristling about her face.

"I'm looking for Jay. They said he was back here someplace," he bluffed.

"You got the wrong building. He's next door with Butterfly and one of the babies today."

Butterfly. Abby's favorite. The one who had taught her about mother love. But something told him that mentioning Abby's name right now would get him booted off the premises without a single answer to his questions.

"Isn't Butterfly the grande dame of Marine Shows?" he said.

"She's been with us for a while," the woman answered cautiously.

"I've heard she's really something. Two live births in captivity, or has there been another since Otto?"

The woman's weathered face broke into a smile as she lowered her guard. "Just the two, though we still use her sometimes when we're training some of the younger ones. She's mostly retired now. She's been with us a long time."

"And Jay's with her now? I've been wanting to meet her for some time now."

"Just don't try introducing yourself," she warned. "She's very selective. She might like you or she might bite you."

"I'll remember that," Matt said. "I can just go out these doors and turn left?"

"That's it. Butterfly's in the old auditorium pool. You'll find Jay either there or back at the nursing pool behind the bleachers with Baby."

"Thank you," he said, pasting on his most charming smile. "I owe you one."

His heart pounded loudly in time with his footsteps as he made his way across the cracked pavement and into the other building. He spotted Jay across the water and quickly circled the slippery edge of the pool. Jay's back was toward him, his concentration on the gray snout protruding from the water.

"Jay?" he said softly, not wanting to interrupt the training session. He wouldn't get any cooperation from the man by antagonizing him.

Jay froze, then turned slowly. "Aw, Christ," he muttered.

"Can you give her a message for me?" Matt said, going straight to the point.

Jay lifted his chin. "Why should I?"

"Tell her I still miss her. Tell her I need to talk to her."

"That all?"

Matt looked away. His gaze scanned the huge open space, seeing nothing but Abby's face in his mind, her eyes smoky with passion before they made love. He closed his eyes and drew a deep breath, then turned back to Jay.

"Tell her I love her."

Jay opened his mouth, then clamped it shut. He bent over and flipped a fish from the bucket into the water. "Okay. Is there someplace she can reach you? If she wants to talk to you, that is. And I'm not saying she does." He stopped, his eyes straying across the water, focusing for a split second on a fixed spot somewhere to the left. "I'll give her a call. Can I walk you out, or can you find your own way?" Jay said, moving in the direction of the double doors.

"She's here." Matt didn't know what made him say

it. He just had a sudden hunch. He followed the direction of Jay's nervous gaze, then walked between the row of bleachers. Through the crisscrossed beams and braces that supported the seats, he could see the rippling water of the nursing pool some forty feet beyond. His lips curved into a smile when he saw a cap of water-slick hair break the surface of the water, followed by the smooth gray snout of a young porpoise.

A gentle laugh floated across the water, a low melodic sound that had haunted Matt's dreams for months. "He did it. Baby did it. We're ready for the hoops now." Abby's voice. Abby's laugh. She really was here.

Matt looked at Jay in triumph. The younger man smiled, though not at him. "Terrific! I'll be right there," Jay called, then glanced at Matt, a resigned expression stealing over his features.

"Let me talk to her first," he said with uncharacteristic sternness. "Understand this, I won't let you upset her. She doesn't need that now. Promise me you'll leave quietly if she doesn't want to see you."

Matt stared at him in silence.

"I'll have you thrown out," Jay added.

But he might as well have been talking to the wind. Matt stepped around him, walking purposefully around the bleachers and toward the nursing pool. He was nearly there when Abby began to climb out. She laughed over her shoulder, then reached back and patted the chattering porpoise beside her. He watched her, the lump in his throat expanding, making it impossible to breathe.

Then she hoisted herself out of the pool and turned sideways, reaching into the ever-present metal bucket. Matt froze in shock as he took in the sight of her. She was pregnant. Very pregnant.

"My God," he whispered.

"I guess it's a shock finding out this way," Jay said flatly, coming up behind him. "I told her a long time ago that she should tell you, but she said you didn't want kids. She said you'd hate her for trapping you. Like she was pulling some kind of a trick on you. Give me a break!"

"So she married someone else? What we had meant so little? Or was she just looking for a man, any man? Maybe it's your baby." Matt knew the words were ugly the minute they left his mouth. But that's how he felt, ugly, cheated, and damned for being a fool.

Jay's fingers curled around Matt's wrist, wiry sinews wrapped around ice-cold flesh. "I ought to flatten your face for that."

"Just try it." Matt heard the fury in his voice, but he couldn't take his eyes off Abby, off the ripeness of the body he'd made love to. A body she'd given to someone else.

"Stop it," Jay said. "Abby's not married."

"Then who's the jerk who—"

"You're the only jerk here," Jay shouted, flinging loose of Matt's arm. Abby looked over then.

For an instant, she stood motionless. For a brief, unguarded instant, he saw sheer pleasure in her eyes, surprised welcome blended with the warmth he remembered. Then anger chased it away.

"What are you doing here?" she said. She splayed a protective hand over her abdomen.

He took three steps toward her, then stopped as a chilling thought took hold. What if the child was his? Stranger things had happened.

Fear slashed through him. His mind flashed back to his mother, her fragile frame ripe with child. His sister, Diane, in her wheelchair, her beautiful smile beaming from her devitalized body. Diane in the oxygen tent. Diane's headstone. Then there was Carrie and that horrible legacy.

Now Abby was pregnant. She'd said she loved him. She'd said she wanted children. She'd said it had been so long, too long since she'd made love. Years.

"My God, what have you done? This wasn't supposed to happen," he said, feeling strangled.

He spun around, fleeing the building as though the hounds of hell were nipping at his heels. He could hear her calling him, her voice cracking. But he couldn't face her now. And he couldn't run away from the horribleness of it all. The fires of hell burned within him, torturing him with the knowledge of what could happen to this unborn child.

Damn, he'd had the vasectomy. But that had been years ago. A memory stole into his ears, Abby's voice whispering that first night together. "Don't worry about it. Vasectomies are reversible. I've even heard of nature reversing it on its own. I'll bet that was a surprise, finding out the little tubes had grown back in place."

My God, he should have told her why. He should have explained about his sister, and then about Carrie. About accidents in the delivery room. About the confusing nightmare of recessive genes that steal lives and ravage dreams.

Matt didn't know how he got to the beach or how far he'd wandered along shore. He was barefoot now, his toes tingling from walking in the cold surf. He vaguely remembered taking off his shoes and carrying them for a while. But he didn't have them now.

He didn't care. Abby Monroe was truly beyond his reach. She left because she was pregnant, because he'd made it plain that fatherhood was not for him.

And it was worse than he could ever have imagined. The child could be his. Probably was his. It had been what, seven and a half months since they'd first made love. Three and a half months since she'd left.

Or maybe the baby wasn't his. It was a hell of a punishment, praying that the woman he loved had betrayed him with another man.

Abby didn't know what a horrible twist of fate that was. She didn't know about defective genes and what they could mean to a helpless child. She didn't know what it was like to love a child and watch it die. He didn't want her to know. He didn't know how to tell her or if he should tell her or hold his silence and simply pray as he never had before.

He felt something tickling his cheek and wiped at it. His fingertips brushed hot moisture. Tears. He slowly lowered his hand, staring at the wet streak across his fingers. He hadn't cried for fifteen years. Not since Carrie died. He stared out at the sea, letting the sun burn into his eyes until he had to shut them against the winter brightness riding low in the sky. Then he turned and walked back, the way he had come.

Up the beach, he spotted a pay phone next to one of the boarded up shacks that dotted this section of the waterfront. Video parlors, T-shirt shops, food stands, go-cart tracks, most closed until the warming temperatures of spring brought the sunbathers back to the beach. He realized before he reached the phone that it was disconnected, the wires probably blown down in a storm. He tried two more before he found one that worked. He dropped in his quarter, tapped out the number, and waited for someone to answer. But he only got their machine.

"Hello, Mom," he said. "I'll be there tonight, as soon as I tie up some business here. Don't make any plans. I need to talk to you and Dad. It's important. I need some advice and—" The closing beep of his parents' answering machine interrupted before he could finish. Slowly, he replaced the receiver. It didn't matter. He could tell them when he got there.

TWELVE

Abby, her father, and Jay had checked every place they could think of, Matt's hotel, the airlines, even the car rental companies. But they'd turned up nothing that could help them find Matt. And Abby wanted very much to find him. She had to.

But this latest idea wasn't panning out either. Her boss had said Matt mentioned visiting his parents at their beach house east of here. She struck out with the local telephone listings. So she'd gone to the library and checked the listings for every beach community between Panama City and Apalachicola. She looked down at the list of telephone numbers and crossed out another. Only a few more left. She punched out the next set of numbers and took a sip of juice while she waited for someone to answer.

"Hello?" The woman's voice was distant and distracted, with the faint warble of age.

Abby swallowed quickly. "Mrs. Gardner?"

"Speaking."

"Is your son Matt there?" Abby asked. It seemed

the most direct way to find out whether she had the right Gardner residence. Last time she'd gotten this far, a six-year-old had come onto the line and told her about his pet turtle.

Soft static that might have been a sigh hissed over the line. "I'm sorry, but Matthew is unable to come to the telephone right now. Could I have him call you?"

"Please," Abby said with a rush of relief. Then she hesitated. "I'm not sure. I'm looking for the Matt Gardner employed by Amusements America. He was at Marine Shows Headquarters yesterday for contract negotiations."

"Is there a problem? I could wake him."

"No, please don't. I just wanted to make sure he's all right. When he left yesterday, he was very upset."

"Who is this?"

Abby drew a deep breath. She didn't know how much Matt had told his family, if anything. "My name is Abby Monroe. I worked with your son in Kansas City last summer."

There was a moment of silence before Matt's mother answered. "Yes, he has mentioned you." Her worried tone indicated he'd done more than mention her.

"Abby," the woman continued, lowering her voice. "I'm going to ask you a very personal question. It may seem like none of my business, but there are medical questions involved."

"I don't understand," Abby said.

"Whose child are you carrying?"

Mrs. Gardner's concise directions led Abby easily to the house, though it wasn't at all what she expected. Tucked away on a side street about a block from the beach, it was as small and unassuming as the rest of the homes in the neighborhood. The distinct pattern of concrete block construction showed beneath the beige paint. Instead of a garage, there was a narrow carport on the west side. Only the vivid green of the postage-stamp front yard labeled it as different from the others. Abby smiled, recognizing the telltale sign of a transplanted Yankee, trying to force Yankee traditions on a climate more suited to palmettos and sandburs.

Abby double-checked the address on the note, then nosed the car into the short crushed-shell drive. She drew a deep breath to gather courage, then stepped out of the car. She shut the door and turned. Her breath hissed through her teeth when Matt stepped out of the shadows of the carport, looking as if he hadn't slept for days. The strain of the last twenty-four hours showed in the pinched set of his lips.

She could barely hear herself think above the pounding of her heart. He'd exchanged yesterday's gray suit for a tattered Rolling Stones T-shirt and jeans that might have been snug six months ago.

A bittersweet wave of longing washed over her, reigniting feelings she'd tried to leave behind with the note she'd left him three months, two weeks, and three nights ago. Only she hadn't been able to forget. The memories had stolen up on her when she least expected it, not just in sleeping dreams, but during the day.

"What are you doing here?" He didn't sound angry, only puzzled.

"Your mother said I could come."

He nodded. "Do you want to go inside and sit down or something? Should you be on your feet?"

Abby smiled thinly. "I'm fine. And before you ask, I'm allowed to drive, swim, and even run, though that's become too uncomfortable."

"You're still working."

Her smile faded as he succinctly brought her back to

her purpose. "About yesterday, I thought I'd better explain in person." She hesitated, still unsure of her reception. Matt's expression wasn't exactly welcoming.

A sturdy woman in a soft pink sweat suit stepped out a side door into the carport. Abby recognized her instantly as a relative of Matt's, probably his mother. She had the same squared forehead and strong jawbone, though her hair was snow white.

Abby held out a hand in greeting. "You must be the lady who gives such excellent directions. I didn't have any trouble finding the place," she rattled on, then caught herself. "Sorry, I'm Abby Monroe."

"And I'm Matthew's mother." The hand that grasped hers was warm and soft.

"You came alone?" Matt asked, coming up behind his mother. He rested a hand lightly on her shoulder, then squeezed.

"I thought it would be best that way. Everyone seems to think I need to be protected."

Mrs. Gardner frowned. "From my son?"

Abby threw up her hands. "From everything. If my father had his way, I'd spend the next month and a half at home drinking milk with my feet propped up on the coffee table.

"Believe me, I understand," Mrs. Gardner said, her expression softening. "Do you need to stretch out a bit or would you rather go inside?"

Abby smiled in nervous relief. She hadn't known what to expect, but this friendly, matter-of-fact woman had eased the worst of her fears with a brief handshake and a welcoming smile. "I'm fine. It's not that long a drive from Panama City," she said. Her eyes strayed restlessly to Matt's face, but his expression remained unreadable.

"So you're feeling all right?" Mrs. Gardner asked.

"I'd be better if this little sea monkey would go back to sleep," Abby admitted as she smoothed a hand across the taut spot where the baby had just kicked again. "She's been doing a tap dance for the last half hour."

The older woman nodded. "One of the many inconveniences of pregnancy," she said. "Matthew was like that, always kicking where it would make me the most uncomfortable. When I was carrying him, I must have spent half my day in the bathroom or running to it."

"Not now, Mom." He squeezed her shoulders.

Abby lifted her chin, meeting Matt's uneasy stare with a soft smile. "On the whole, it seems a small sacrifice," she said. "Not nearly as much as other things I've given up."

"I agree." Mrs. Gardner took her hand. "I just wanted a word with you."

"Leave it alone, Mom. This doesn't involve you."

The woman's probing gaze disturbed Abby, demanding something undefined. Abby looked away, absently registering the details of her surroundings, the gray pencil sticks of the leafless young trees in the front yard, the row of sand dollars drying on a sheltered windowsill.

"I just want to explain. I think I owe Matt that much," Abby said. "After we've cleared the air, I'll go. I've done enough damage already."

Matt scuffed the toe of his shoe in the crushed shells, then smiled with reluctant admiration. "We make our own luck. When you said that, I didn't realize how literally you meant it. You certainly know how to take control of your life." He shook his head and turned away, leaning on the car hood.

Abby tapped against her thigh, then clenched her hands together in front of her to stop the nervous movement. This was awkward. She didn't know where to begin. Or how. It might have been easier if they were alone. But they weren't, and Mrs. Gardner seemed firmly planted on the spot. Abby leaned back against the car and started with the problem uppermost in her mind.

"Yesterday, you said this wasn't supposed to happen. I need to explain about this baby. This is *my* child. Not yours. Not some other man's. Just mine." She glanced from one to the other, unsure of how to proceed.

The older woman's lines rearranged themselves into an expression of helpless acceptance, though the deeper marks of pain shone from her liquid-brown eyes. "I told him everything you told me. I know it's none of my business. But I couldn't let him go on thinking that . . ."

"Mother!"

"I couldn't let you think that you'd harmed this woman. You're my child. I couldn't let you suffer any more." She shook her head, then turned and slowly walked away.

"Harmed me?" Abby felt even more confused.

Mrs. Gardner reached the door, then hesitated an instant. "Please understand. His daughter's death hurt him, Abby. It made us all very bitter and very careful," she said.

It took a moment for Abby to absorb the shock. "Daughter? You had a child?"

Mrs. Gardner's eyes widened. "You didn't tell her?" A heavy sigh escaped her. "I wonder if you two ever really talked."

"A daughter?" Her first thought was for herself. She felt lied to, though she knew the error was one of omission. But heavy guilt settled quickly over the sense of betrayal. The omission was no greater than her own.

He caught her hand. "Let's go someplace private. There are too many people around here. Heck, half the neighborhood is probably peeking through the curtains and speculating about us already."

"Inside?" she suggested.

"Are you up to a short walk?"

"I'm pregnant, not crippled," she reminded him, pulling her hand away.

"Right." He locked his hands behind his back, walking stiffly beside her as they left the driveway. They walked the short distance to the beach in silence. It wasn't until they sprinted across the two-lane highway that they spoke again.

"Are you all right?" Matt demanded when Abby stopped and grunted.

"Fine. She just got a little excited and kicked a little harder than usual." She rubbed her hand over the spot again. "She's very active. I think the donor must have been a kick-boxer or something."

Matt looked slightly uncomfortable. "How much do you know about this donor?"

"Very little, actually," Abby said, starting over the low dune of dirty-white sand. This time, she didn't resist when he took her hand but allowed him to help her along the slippery path.

"His identify is in the clinic's files somewhere," she continued. "But they blacked out the name on the copy of the medical history they gave me. It's best that way, I suppose. He can't find me. I can't find him. Under the circumstances I wouldn't have it any other way."

Matt stopped at the crest of the dune and looked out over the water. "I suppose that so long as you have the medical records it doesn't matter."

"That was important to me."

He glanced down at her. "I think you were right." He pointed out across the water. "That spit of land out there is St. Joseph Peninsula, and that cloud of smoke to the left is the paper mill. We're lucky, the breeze is blowing the smell away today."

"Sunshine and a favorable breeze. What more could we ask for?" She started down the path ahead of him. She walked out to the water, stopping at the edge of the foaming surf. They had the beach to themselves for the moment, although she could see a couple walking along the water's edge in the distance.

"The water's calm today," she commented when he came up beside her. "Or is it always that way?"

"The peninsula protects the bay, but you're right about its being calm. Must be between tides."

They let the silence fall between them again as they followed the course of a small shrimp boat across the bay. Finally, Matt spoke.

"I didn't lie when I said I'd never been married. And I don't have any living children. I've just never been able to talk about Carrie."

"Please," Abby whispered, looking up at him. "I need to understand."

"I guess you do." He drew a deep breath, then caught her hand and led her to a washed up timber about ten feet beyond the reach of the surf.

He settled close to her, still grasping her hand, though Abby doubted he realized he still held it. He looked far away, lost in memories he'd rather keep locked away.

"We were both young, still in college," he said. "But we were smart enough to know better than to compound one mistake with another. And as it turned out, we were right not to get married simply because we were having a baby."

At least that was one point they agreed upon, Abby thought, though she didn't think now was the time to say so.

"By the time it was all over, we couldn't even speak to one another. It was awful."

"What happened?"

Matt shook his head. "The baby died." She could tell by the way his eyes avoided hers that he was holding something back.

"How did the baby die?"

"I shouldn't have started this. It's a very long and complicated story. Not something a pregnant woman needs to hear."

"Why? I don't need to be protected. I'm the same person I've always been, just a little bigger."

"I'm not going to sit here and tell you what can go wrong. You don't need to hear that now."

She touched his cheek, turning his face until she could see into his eyes. "You couldn't scare me any more than I've scared myself. Every pregnant woman has this secret fear that something might be wrong with her baby. I know that things go wrong. But I've had tests, and this baby is fine. Why are you so afraid?"

His laugh was harsh and bitter sounding. "Me, afraid? Abby, when you came up out of that pool, you scared the living hell out of me. I actually prayed that you'd been sleeping around the entire time you were with me. Because that would be better than the possibility of a vasectomy failure."

"Matt?" He looked so pale, almost gray-faced. Like yesterday. This strange intensity frightened her.

"It started with my sister," he said.

Abby frowned. "You said she died young."

Matt sighed. "She had cerebral palsy. It was pretty severe, or at least it seemed bad to a kid like me. She seemed to be getting better with the help of the physical therapy and the new medicine. But, she caught the flu and ended up with pneumonia. She just didn't have the strength to fight it."

"And then there was Carrie."

"Your child?"

He turned red-rimmed eyes on her. "I was twenty-one when she was born and twenty-one when she died. What kind of justice is there in a world where kids like that are born without even a chance at living? She lived for only five weeks. She had a chromosomal disorder called trisomy 18."

Abby squeezed his hand. She could imagine what an impact this would have on someone so young, especially one who had already witnessed the death of his sister. A double blow with lifelong repercussions. It was a horrible coincidence of nature, like something you read about in the newspapers but figure will never happen to anyone you know.

"You couldn't stand to lose another child," she whispered. She wasn't sure that she wouldn't feel the same under the circumstances.

"That's part of it. But this disease. The babies are so deformed that they can't survive. They always die, some soon and others after a year or so. And I'm a carrier."

She looked up at him, so strong and healthy. "You're sure?"

"It's caused by a recessive gene. Both parents have to be carriers. So you see, I'm very, very sure. The doctors said that when both parents are carriers, they have about a one in four chance of having a child with the disease. Otherwise, the defective gene can pass on from one generation to the next like some sort of time bomb. So I had to be certain that my part in it ended here with me."

"And that explains the vasectomy," she said. She squeezed his hand hard, using the physical pressure as a focal point while she forced back her own tears. "I wish it could have been something more selfish, like you just hated kids. Or you thought I was too ugly to be the mother of *your* child."

He laughed. This time it was a release, a shedding of the tension that gripped him. "You're nuts, you know that?" He pulled her close, holding her carefully, as if the extra bulk between them might pop if he hugged too tightly.

"Abby love, we've wasted so much time," he said with a catch in his voice.

Abby stilled. "What do you mean?"

His hands skimmed up her arms to cup her face. "If there had been no baby and no secrets, what would have been your answer when I asked you to marry me?"

Abby didn't have to think about that. She'd always known he was more than other men. "It would have been yes. But there was the baby. There still is."

"I love the baby, too," he said. "It's a part of you."

Abby squeezed her eyes closed. "If you had known about the baby before, would you have asked me to marry you?"

She felt the soft brush of his lips on hers, and it was all she could do to keep her body from molding itself instinctively against him.

"That's no answer," she whispered, forcing her eyes open.

"You didn't give me the option of deciding for myself."

She pulled away from him and stood. She paced the sand in front of him, torn again by the decision she'd made. She stopped suddenly in front of him and crossed her arms. "I couldn't do it," she said. "I loved you too much to tie you into a situation you didn't choose. You don't want a child, and I've always known you had a strong reason, something that hurt you badly."

"That's a very noble attitude. But what gives you the right to make that choice for me?"

Abby lifted her chin. "I did what I thought was best. Maybe it was a mistake. But it's too late to change that."

"But it's not too late to start over."

"Start over? Are you kidding?" she asked incredulously. "I'm six weeks away from motherhood. That means there's a basketball-sized bulge between us when we hug and a squirming, kicking fetus keeping me awake when I try to sleep. Then there will be diapers and feedings in the middle of the night, followed by teething, the terrible twos, and a college education bill."

Matt nodded, rising from his seat. "As long as it's with you, it's everything I want. Sometime before dawn I realized that I love you enough to see you through anything, even the birth of a child like Carrie."

Abby frowned. "This baby is fine. I know. I've had tests, and something like that would have shown up."

He nodded. "Since it isn't mine, there's nothing to worry about," he said. He touched her face. "Just for the record, if things had been different, I would have given my soul to have a child with you."

"But they aren't different. You aren't different. You don't have to do this. I was prepared to be a single mother long before I met you. I have a nice little inheritance from my aunt to pay for the bigger expenses, and I make a decent living."

"A baby needs a father."

"My baby has a whole family of male role models."

"I need you," he told her. "I need your laughter and your love. You said before that you loved me. Do you still? Do you love me enough to let me back into your life?"

Abby wanted so much to believe him, to trust that her instincts were correct. He looked at her with a mixture of love and deep yearning.

"Maybe you're in love with the idea of having a family when you thought you would never have one," she argued.

He flung out his arms in frustration. "What do I have to do to convince you? Write it in the sand in blood? Shout it so the whole neighborhood can hear?"

He ran up toward the path over the low dune.

"Matt, what are you doing?"

He stopped at the crest. "I love Abby Monroe," he shouted. "I love Abby Monroe and I want to marry her."

He spun back around, facing her. "Abby, will you marry me? Today, tomorrow, next week? Name the date."

"You're crazy!" she shouted back.

"Crazy in love since the day we met. Now are you going to marry me before I make an even bigger fool of myself?"

Abby stared for a moment, then turned away, looking to the ocean for answers. She didn't want to be an obligation, but she was very much afraid that was what prompted this proposal. That and the sudden relief over her explanation about her baby.

But she loved him, too much to let him go a second

time. He'd loved her in September. And just yesterday, he'd told Jay that he loved her. And that was before he knew about the baby.

Her head still argued with doubts and logic. But her heart recognized the truth. Matt loved *her*.

She spun back around. "Yes," she shouted.

He spread his arms and yelled so loudly the entire county must have heard. Abby had to laugh, though it was more from joy and excitement than amusement at Matt's wild dance down the path.

"Baby girl, you're going to have a daddy after all," she said softly as Matt rushed to her.

He caught her up in his arms and spun her around. Then he gently lowered her to the sand.

"You're mine," he said. "Both of you." He laid both hands on her rounded belly, caressing gently until he felt the baby's kick. She thought she saw a glimmer of tears in his eyes as he absorbed the gentle bump of her child against his fingertips.

"And you're ours," Abby replied. "For always." She rose to her knees to touch his lips. This time, his kiss was more than tenderness. It held a promise of passion to come, of a new beginning.

He sank back, pulling her into his lap. "Come here. I want to hold you and tell you all the things I'm going to do with you when there's no wriggling basketball between us."

"And maybe I'll tell you what we can do now." She leaned forward, whispering in his ear. "Much more than you'd think. You see, I have this book."

SHARE THE FUN . . .
SHARE YOUR NEW-FOUND TREASURE!!

You don't want to let your new books out of your sight? That's okay. Your friends can get their own. Order below.

No. 22 NEVER LET GO by Laura Phillips
Ryan has a big dilemma. Kelly is the answer to *all* his prayers.

No. 40 CATCH A RISING STAR by Laura Phillips
Justin is seeking fame; Beth helps him find something more important.

No. 78 TO LOVE A COWBOY by Laura Phillips
Dee is the dark-haired beauty that sends Nick reeling back to the past.

No. 99 MOON SHOWERS by Laura Phillips
Both Sam and the historic Missouri home quickly won Hilary's heart.

No. 110 BEGINNINGS by Laura Phillips
Abby had her future completely mapped out—until Matt showed up.

No. 68 PROMISE OF PARADISE by Karen Lawton Barrett
Gabriel is surprised to find that Eden's beauty is not just skin deep.

No. 69 OCEAN OF DREAMS by Patricia Hagan
Is Jenny just another shipboard romance to Officer Kirk Moen?

No. 70 SUNDAY KIND OF LOVE by Lois Faye Dyer
Trace literally sweeps beautiful, ebony-haired Lily off her feet.

No. 71 ISLAND SECRETS by Darcy Rice
Chad has the power to take away Tucker's hard-earned independence.

No. 72 COMING HOME by Janis Reams Hudson
Clint always loved Lacey. Now Fate has given them another chance.

No. 73 KING'S RANSOM by Sharon Sala
Jesse was always like King's little sister. When did it all change?

No. 74 A MAN WORTH LOVING by Karen Rose Smith
Nate's middle name is 'freedom' . . . that is, until Shara comes along.

No. 75 RAINBOWS & LOVE SONGS by Catherine Sellers
Dan has more than one problem. One of them is named Kacy!

No. 76 ALWAYS ANNIE by Patty Copeland
Annie is down-to-earth and real . . . and Ted's never met anyone like her.

No. 77 FLIGHT OF THE SWAN by Lacey Dancer
Rich had decided to swear off romance for good until Christiana.

No. 79 SASSY LADY by Becky Barker
No matter how hard he tries, Curt can't seem to get away from Maggie.